THE NEW MISTRESS AT THE
CHALET SCHOOL

Other titles by Elinor M. Brent-Dyer in Armada include

The School at the Chalet
The Chalet School in Exile
Eustacia Goes to the Chalet School
Peggy of the Chalet School
Mary-Lou at the Chalet School
The Chalet School and Jo
Three Go to the Chalet School
The New House at the Chalet School
Shocks for the Chalet School
The Princess of the Chalet School
The Chalet School and the Island
The Chalet School and Barbara
The Coming of Age of the Chalet School
A Problem for the Chalet School
A Rebel at the Chalet School

First published in the U.K. in 1957 by
W. & R. Chambers Ltd., London and Edinburgh.
This edition was first published in Armada in 1969 by
Fontana Paperbacks,
14 St. James's Place, London SW1A 1PS.

This impression 1982.

© Elinor M. Brent-Dyer 1957.

Printed in Great Britain by
Love & Malcomson Ltd.,
Brighton Road, Redhill, Surrey.

THE NEW MISTRESS AT THE CHALET SCHOOL

Elinor M. Brent-Dyer

Armada

CONTENTS

Chapter I

"THE DREAM OF MY LIFE!"

"KATHIE—Kathie! *Yoo-hoo!*"

The clear call rang through the house and there came the sound of the hurried opening of a door followed by quick footsteps and then a smooth brown head, gleaming in the sunlight which poured through the landing-window at the head of the stairs, appeared over the banisters.

"Auntie! You've got back awfully quickly. I'll be down in a minute, and coffee's all ready on the simmering-plate."

"You'll be down quicker than that, my lady!" Mrs. Grayson said. "There's a letter for you on the hall-table. Come down and collect. The postmark is—Switzerland!"

"Switzerland!" The head was promptly withdrawn and the next moment, Kathie Ferrars was flying down the short flight of stairs, brown eyes aglow with excitement. "Where is it? Give it to me! Oh, I *won*-der!" Her voice trailed off as her aunt put the letter into her eager hand and she stood looking down at it in silence.

Mrs. Grayson removed the shady hat she had worn against the brilliant June sun, smoothed down her wavy hair and then turned to look at her niece with a humorous quirk of her lips. "Well! Aren't you going to open it?"

Kathie looked up at her. "I—I'm almost afraid to. I've wanted it so much. Suppose this is just to say that someone else has got the job?"

"Come into the drawing-room and open it. You can tell me what they say when I bring the coffee."

With a sudden childish gesture, Kathie thrust the letter at her aunt. *"You* open it, Auntie! I'll go and get the coffee."

"Oh, Kathie! Be your age—do!" Mrs. Grayson spoke with good-humoured exasperation as she pushed the letter back to its owner. Open it and don't be so silly!"

Kathie went red. She knew well enough that, at twenty-two, it was high time she had got over these babyish fits. A young woman of her age who had got her B.A. and was preparing to go out into the world to earn her own

5

living must learn to face whatever might come along, whether of good or ill. She tore the letter open and extracted the contents in silence. A long, folded affair with a note inside appeared. She dropped the first on to the hall table and glanced at the latter.

"Dear Miss Ferrars,
    I write to offer you the post of form mistress to the Intermediate Fifth Form in this school, together with some Junior mathematics and geography in your own form and the two top forms of Middle School."

There was more of it, but that was all she saw just then. Her eyes lighted up afresh and she gave vent to a low chuckle. She had got it! The one post of all that she most wanted! It was almost too good to be believed!

Mrs. Grayson, standing at the door, her blue eyes dancing with sympathetic amusement, joined in the chuckle. "Good news, then?"

"I've *got* it!" Kathie said deeply.

"Excellent! I'm very glad indeed! Now I'll go and get that coffee. Shan't be a minute! "

Left alone, Kathie smoothed out the letter and read it to the end. Then she turned to the enclosure. When her aunt came bearing a tray with two cups of coffee and a plate of cream biscuits, she looked up at her with a face alight with pleasure. "Oh, Auntie! Doesn't it seem almost too good to be true! "

"You tell me exactly what you have to do and I'll see if I agree with you," her aunt said cautiously.

"I'm to take Intermediate Fifth—girls whose ages range between thirteen and fifteen and who are not quite ready for the advance work of Fifth proper but who are beyond Upper IVa which is the top form in Middle School. I'll teach them maths., some English, and geography. I've also to take maths. in the two Upper IV's and most of *their* geography. Term begins on 20th September, but the staff go two days earlier for Staff Meeting and to arrange about escort duty for the girls. Oh, and I'm in Ste Thérèse House. All the Houses are named after various woman saints, you know. Miss Wilson told me that when I went for interview."

"And Miss Wilson is Head?" Mrs. Grayson asked.

"One of them. There are two—Miss Wilson and Miss Annersley. I don't know which is the real boss or if they're both equal. The school really belongs to a limited company, headed by Lady Russell who founded it ages ago."

"Lady Russell? That name rings a bell somewhere," Mrs. Grayson said.

"I expect you've heard Uncle talk of Sir James Russell. Isn't he one of the big men on T.B.? She's his wife and she started the school in Tirol long before she married him. Now, it's such a big affair, that they've turned it into a limited liability company and quite a lot of people have shares in it. But Lady Russell is still head of it or chairman or whatever they call it," Kathie explained.

"When did you hear all this?" her aunt demanded, sitting up in her chair.

"Oh, Miss Wilson told me," Kathie replied carelessly.

"And you never told me! Oh, Kathie, what a little idiot you are! If you'd only let me know, I could have told you you'd no need to worry about whether you'd got the post or not. For I don't imagine for a moment she would have gone into such details with anyone she didn't intend to engage."

"I never thought about it," her niece replied, looking blank.

"Oh, well, it's over now. But I wonder your own common sense didn't tell you."

Kathie laughed. "But darling! You're always telling me I haven't any!"

"No, and it's high time you developed a little. Remember, you're about to be responsible for a group of girls who ought to look up to you. You'll have to make decisions for them and help them to right choices. Your work isn't just teaching, you know. If you do things rightly, you help to form their characters. You'll have to grow up a little, my child. It's my fault, of course. I've kept you a baby too long. I'm sorry, Kathie. Somehow I forgot how quickly the years go and I *didn't* want to lose my little girl. Can you forgive me?"

Kathie tumbled out of her chair and on to her knees beside the woman who had been mother to her ever since the day when they had laid the motherless and fatherless day-old baby in her arms.

"Auntie darling! There's nothing to forgive! It's me myself. It's been so easy to hang on to you and Uncle Frank and let you make all the decisions for me. I knew

7

all right if I said I wanted to do it myself you'd agree, but I've always been afraid of making stupid mistakes.

"Yes," Mrs. Grayson said. "Perhaps if you had really been our own girl, I might have hardened my heart. I was afraid, too—afraid of making you feel even the slightest difference."

"It wouldn't have done that," Kathie said. "No father and mother could ever have meant more to me than you and Uncle do. But I'll turn over a new leaf. I'll start in by choosing all my clothes for this beginning and I won't ask you about a single thing. And if I make mistakes, I'll stand by them. They'll be *my* mistakes, anyhow! "

"All your clothes?" Mrs. Grayson looked mischievous.

"I'll have to have a new suit and some jumpers and a winter coat—oh, and quite a lot of other things. Miss Wilson told me the winters can be bitterly cold so high up in the Alps. I expect I'll need quite a lot of things. Luckily, my dividends come in July so I'll have plenty of money for all I want. It'll mean spending this time, but I shouldn't need to get anything for the spring term and I had new frocks this summer. And then there'll be my salary besides."

Mrs. Grayson asked to see the contract. Kathie handed it to her and she scanned it thoughtfully.

"Very business-like," she commented as she returned it. "You can sign it tonight after dinner when we'll hope Uncle will be in and you can post it tomorrow. Now get up and don't stay kneeling there, you goose! You'll have to calm down a little as well as everything else. As form mistress of—what is it—Intermediate Fifth? Well, you can't be flying up at every excuse. A fine example that would be for your pupils. You must try to develop a little more dignity, my child."

Kathie laughed as she got up. "Oh, I know. But when you've wanted something tremendously and then find you've got it, it *is* rather exciting. But I really will try to be dignified and grown-up from now on. I *must*, of course."

"You stick to that," Mrs. Grayson said cordially. "Especially considering the age of the girls in your form. It's always a tiresome age. You'll have to watch your step, Kathie, and don't give them any excuse for not respecting you."

"I'll watch Miss Wilson and imitate her. I liked her

8

awfully, but I can't imagine anyone taking the least liberty with her."

"My dear girl, she would hardly be in her present post if there were any risk of that." Mrs. Grayson had risen and she stood looking down at the glowing face she loved. She was a tall woman and Kathie was barely average height. Suddenly she bent and kissed the girl. "I'm very glad you've got it. I hope you'll be happy in your work and make good."

"I ought to after all you and Uncle Frank have done for me. And from what Nell Randolph told me, the Chalet School really is a marvellous place."

"Why didn't Nell try for the job herself?" Mrs. Grayson asked.

"Oh, she wants to be near her mother. Mrs. Randolph is delicate and Nell is all she has. Switzerland would have been much too far away. Nell's got a job at the other branch, though, at Carnbach on the South Wales coast. Mrs. Randolph had the chance of a small house there, so Nell will be able to live at home and go daily. And there's another thing. Miss Annersley, the other Head at the Görnetz Platz, is a cousin of Nell's. I rather think that's another reason why she didn't put in for the job. It wouldn't be much fun to have a relative for your Head. She'd know a lot too much about you!"

"Were there any Chalet School girls at Oxford?" Mrs. Grayson asked.

"Two—Mollie Carew and Joan Sandys, but they were both Second Years when Nell and I were Freshers. We didn't know them awfully well. But they were very nice. There weren't any in our year. Nell said that most of them had gone on to the finishing branch in Switzerland. She had a term there, but she had to leave then, because her mother was ill. I always thought it was hard luck on her, but it couldn't be helped. I'd have done the same if it had been you."

"Thank you, dear. I'm sure you would. And now I must go and see to lunch or Uncle will be arriving and find nothing ready. Put that contract away safely till tonight and go and lay a table, will you, and don't forget anything in your excitement." Mrs. Grayson laughed comfortably before she concluded, "And just make up your mind to assume a little dignity, even if it doesn't come naturally as yet. Tomorrow, we must go into the

9

question of clothes. September isn't so very far away and you'll find a good deal to do, especially when you take out three weeks in Devonshire next month! "

"But I *can* practise being dignified all the time," Kathie laughed as she laid the contract away in the sécrétaire at the other end of the room.

"'By all means! That's a very good idea! '" Mrs. Grayson departed kitchenwards while her niece went to lay the table in the sunny dining-room, revolving plans for assuming very grown-up ways and manners as she worked. Her aunt's advice had been well-meant and certainly part of it was needed, but the emphasis she had laid on it was to prove a mistake and the source of future trouble to the girl she loved so dearly.

Chapter II

MISS O'RYAN

KATHIE sat in the train that was taking her to Paddington. She had to meet Miss o'Ryan, history mistress at the Chalet School, at Victoria by ten o'clock. A long letter had arrived from the Görnetz Platz the previous week, giving her all instructions and she was bound to admit that the writer, who signed herself "Rosalie Dene (School Secretary)" seemed to have thought of everything.

"I wonder," she thought as she sat staring out at the flying landscape, "what Miss o'Ryan is like? Irish, from her name. She sounds rather decent from Miss Dene's letter. What was it she said about her?"

She fished in her handbag for the letter and skimmed it through for the twentieth time.

"Just in case there should be any difficulty, wear a sprig of heather on the lapel of your coat and look out for someone your own age or thereabouts wearing the same. Miss o'Ryan is small and very pretty, with the bluest eyes and masses of black hair.

"I hope to goodness she finds me," Kathie thought as she folded up the letter and returned it to her bag.

At Paddington, she had no trouble at all. A pleasant young porter took charge of her and the suitcase she had

10

with her—her trunk had been sent off last week—and put her into a taxi. The taxi landed her at the main entrance to Victoria station and an elderly porter this time took her under his wing and deposited her and her belongings at the big bookstall in the station hall.

A glance at the station clock told her that she had five minutes to spare so she turned her attention to the bookstall. Someone touched her arm and she whirled round to find herself facing another girl, shorter than herself and so startlingly pretty that she nearly gasped. This was quite clearly Miss o'Ryan. Kathie knew that even before she spoke.

"I'm sure 'tis our new mistress, Miss Ferrars," said a lilting voice with just the faintest touch of creamy Irish brogue. "I'm Miss o'Ryan—Biddy o'Ryan."

Kathie forgot her shyness. "I'm Kathie Ferrars," she said simply. "It's awfully good of you to meet me and—and show me the ropes like this, Miss o'Ryan."

"Sure, you couldn't be expecting anyone to let you take this long journey alone for the first time," Miss o'Ryan told her with a laugh as lilting as her speaking voice. "Well, shall we be moving to take our seats? Have you got all you want to read? 'Tis a long journey, but you'll be sleeping part of tonight, anyway, I hope. I'll show you how to make yourself really comfy. I'm an old and seasoned traveller!" She laughed again. Then she looked at the little pile of luggage between them. "Is this everything?"

"Yes, my trunk went in advance," Kathie explained. "I had a letter telling me to do that and it went halfway through last week."

"Then 'twill be waiting for you all right. Do you want any magazines—or papers?"

"No, thank you. I've a book and some magazines in my attaché case."

Miss o'Ryan beamed and two dimples dipped in her cheeks. "Then come and we'll settle in and be comfy before the rush comes. This way!" And she led the way to the boat-train platform with an air of certainty that impressed Kathie enormously.

"I always think it as well to travel as light as possible," she said as they reached the long train standing waiting at the platform. "This is the ferry train and it goes straight through to the Gare du Nord; but we've got to

11

cross Paris to the Gare de l'Est and we ought to try to get some sort of meal before we board the Basle train."

"I thought we fed on the train?" Kathie remarked.

"Oh, yes; dinner, of course. And lunch going to Paris. But I like something in the afternoon. We'll find a pâtisserie somewhere and have coffee and cakes before we go on. We don't leave Paris till six o'clock or thereabouts."

"When do we reach Basle?" Kathie asked curiously as she followed her cicerone along the platform.

"Six-thirty tomorrow morning. Breakfast at the station and then we'll go to the garage where Rosalie—Miss Dene, I mean—said she would leave the runabout for us. We're picking up two other people at Basle, by the way; Miss Burnett who is our Games mistress, and Miss Andrews who teaches the babies. You'll like them. Miss Andrews can't be much older than you and Miss Burnett is about the same age. They're a jolly pair and great chums. They've been spending the last fortnight of the hols with one of our Old Girls who was at school with Peggy Burnett in the Dark Ages—Marie Drooglever. The Drooglevers live in Leyden and those two will have had a glorious time if I know Marie. Here's our coach. I came here first and parked my belongings before I came to hunt you up. Come along—just down here."

She brought them up short and proceeded to help Kathie put her case in the rack and pile her attaché case and handbag and book on the little table already set up. They sat down and she beamed again at her new acquaintance.

"Now we're set until we reach Paris. I've ordered coffee and biscuits for eleven o'clock. That suit you?"

Kathie assented as she took her seat. This journey had been rather a nightmare to such an untried traveller, but Miss o'Ryan was taking charge of everything so competently that her companion felt the last terror slip away. She snuggled comfortably into her seat and prepared to enjoy it after all.

Miss o'Ryan opened her case and brought out a book, *The Times*, a knitting bag and a box of American candies. Then she looked across at Kathie and laughed.

"I told you 'twas a seasoned traveller I am. Try one of these candies and let's talk. I've strict instructions to answer all your questions as far as I can, that way you won't be feeling too strange when school begins. I've cigarettes in my bag if you'd rather," she added, producing them. "Maybe, though, you don't smoke?"

"Not very much," Kathie owned. "I like one now and then, but I'd rather have one of these luscious things now, thank you."

They sat munching companionably, and Kathie rather shyly asked one or two questions, mainly about the girls. Miss o'Ryan replied amiably.

"You'll find our girls are very decent as girls go," she said. "Of course, if they think you're going to be soft with them, they'll have a shot at playing you up. But if you let them see you'll be standing no nonsense, they'll pipe down. We have our share of young demons, but the general feeling in the school is that certain things aren't done and anyone who tries to do them gets it in the neck from her little playmates. The thing to do is to let them see just how far they may go with you and stick to it. Don't try to pull the reins too tight. That only means that sooner or later there's a bolt and that does nobody any good."

Kathie looked puzzled. "It doesn't sound awfully easy," she said. "I mean you say I must be firm and then you tell me not to pull the reins too tight. How does one manage?"

"Make up your mind just how far you intend to let them go and don't make it too rigid a line," Biddy replied. "But once you've set your line, stick to it unless anything happens which makes it look wiser to relax a little. You'll soon find out for yourself. My own theory is that you can only learn that sort of thing by experience."

The talk stopped after that. Miss o'Ryan buried herself in *The Times* crossword and Kathie opened her book. The coffee arrived and they enjoyed it, but Miss o'Ryan kept off the school. Instead, she consulted the new mistress about one or two teasers in her crossword. Kathie rarely bothered with them, but she had a keen brain and gave her mind seriously to the problems.

They arrived at Paris without incident and Biddy o'Ryan escorted the new mistress across the gay, busy city to the Gare de l'Est where they left their cases in charge of a porter to whom, the history mistress spoke in rapid, fluent French, much to the admiration of Kathie whose own French was fluent enough, but distinctly with a "Stratford-atte-Bow" accent. Miss o'Ryan sounded like a native.

"I say! You do speak French well!" she said when they

13

were seeking for their pâtisserie for coffee and cakes.

"Of course! We've always prided ourselves on being trilingual at the Chalet."

"Did you find it awfully hard to teach in other languages at first?" Kathie asked curiously, for this was something that had been troubling her.

"How could I? I was accustomed to being *taught* in them." Then, as she saw the bewildered look on her companion's face, Biddy explained, "Sure, have you never understood that I'm an Old Girl of the Chalet School? I was there when it was in Tirol in the Dark Ages. I was there during our first years in England, when we had to leave the Tiern See, thanks to old Hitler. I took another job when my university career ended—well, it was wished on to me in one way. But it took me out to Australia for a year or two. But as soon as it came to an end, I shot home and begged a job at my own school. And there I've been ever since. And," she added, "however much I may leave as a mistress, I'll always be a Chalet girl."

"Leave? Are you leaving then?" Kathie asked innocently

She was startled at the deep blush that swept across her companion's charming face. "Not till next summer. But then—well, 'tis married I'm hoping to be then."

"Oh!" It was all Kathie said, but she felt a sudden disappointment. She liked this Irish girl already and she had been hoping they would be together for the next two or three years. It was a shock to hear that Miss o'Ryan had other plans for the future.

Biddy paused and led the way into a big pâtisserie, but she said no more until they were seated at their table with cups of delicious coffee and plates loaded with cakes and pastries they had selected themselves from the heaped-up trays. Then, as Kathie took the first sip of her coffee, she said simply. "'Tis not so far away I'll be, even when I'm married. He's one of the doctors at the big Sanatorium at the other end of the Platz and our home will be up there. In fact," she added, laughing, "there's quite a colony of us there already. A number of us Old Girls have come back to the school to teach and, as you'll be finding, a good many of us have married doctors. Now there's going to be me—I'm marrying Herr Doktor Courvoisier whom we met through a ghastly accident when we had the girls down in Lucerne one expedition. And, of course, there's

14

Joey herself. She's married to Jack Maynard who is head of the San staff and they live next door to the school. They," she added with wickedly dancing eyes, "have quite a family. There are nine little Maynards now since Cecil arrived at Easter."

"Nine?" Kathie gasped. "Oh, *no!* "

"It's 'Oh yes', me dear! " Biddy retorted. "Len, Con and Margot Maynard are all pupils at the Chalet School and Felicity will be coming as soon as she's old enough. She's one of the twins," she added in parenthesis. "Cecil's only five months old at the moment, but she's slated for the school, too."

"Five girls? Four boys, then?" Kathie asked.

Biddy nodded. "Three singletons, Stephen, Charles and Michael. Then Felix who is Felicity's twin. By the way, Len and Con will be in your form. They're nearly thirteen now."

"Both of them? Are there two lots of twins, then?"

"No; only Felix and Felicity." Then, as she saw the sheer bewilderment in Kathie's face, Biddy relented. "Len, Con and Margot were the first and they're triplets. It was just like Joey. She always had done things in a wholesale way, the creature! If she'd been content with one at a time the way most folk are, she'd have only six. But she began with triplets and Felix and Felicity came along three years ago. They were three at the beginning of this month."

"Oh, I see." Kathie giggled. "It was rather a shock, I must say. By the way, you said that Len and Con—what are their proper names?—would be in my form. Why not Margot as well?"

"Len is Helena and Con is Constance. As for young Margot, partly 'tis laziness but partly 'tis her health. When she was little she was so frail that no one ever thought they'd rear her. I remember," Biddy went on reminiscently, "Joey saying to me once, 'If she's to have only a short time in this world, I want it to be a happy one'. So no one made much fuss when Margot slacked and dawdled. When she was nine, though, they sent her to Canada with her aunt, Lady Russell—our Madame— and she's never looked back since then. There's not a trace of delicacy about her now. 'Twas the dry cold of the Canadian winters did the trick. Only, by that time, you see, she'd got into the way of taking life easily and she hadn't

15

any real foundations. So every now and then, she doesn't know and other things slide. She's had a hard time of it, trying to pull up, the poor creature, but she's making headway now. The other two will have to pull up their socks, for once she's level with them, she'll be cleverest of the family—so far."

Kathie nodded. "I see. And are Len and Con clever, too?"

"Len is; and a real student. She revels in her lessons. Con—well Con is out of the ordinary. She's the one that's inherited her mother's gift and some day she's going to blossom forth as a writer."

"Does Mrs. Maynard write, then?" Kathie queried. "What name does she write under? What sort of books does she write?"

"Juveniles and historical fiction, mainly. She writes under her maiden name. Oh, you'll know her books all right," Biddy said confidently. "You've read *King's Soldiermaid* and *Swords Crossed*, haven't you?"

"But my dear! I simply love her books! I read all her school stories—in fact, I've gone *on* reading them. I have the lot and all the novels as well. And you say she lives next door to the school?"

"At Freudesheim," Biddy nodded. "You'll be seeing plenty of her, once we've settled down for the term."

"Does she teach, then?"

"She does not. Give the poor girl a chance! With a house, a husband, a long family and her books, where do you think she'd find time for teaching?"

"Then how can I be seeing a lot of her?" Kathie demanded.

"Because however many activities she may have, Joey is and always will be a Chalet School girl. I sometimes think," Biddy continued as she set down her empty coffee-cup, "that she's the spirit of all the school is and hopes to be. But I'm saying no more. You must find it out for yourself. At the present moment, might I be reminding you that we've a train to catch? If we miss it, we'll miss Staff meeting and then no one's going to love us very much."

"Oh, mercy! I don't want that to happen!" Kathie bolted the rest of her cake and drained her coffee and they fled.

16

Chapter III

ARRIVAL IN BASLE

KATHIE stirred uneasily and murmured in her sleep. Miss o'Ryan spoke her name and shook her gently. This had no effect, so the history mistress shook her most *un*gently.

"Miss Ferrars! Wake up! We're nearly into Basle! Mercy, how the woman sleeps! *Miss Ferrars!* *Wake up!*" This last was literally bawled and Kathie woke up with a start and stared wildly round her. Her eyes encountered Biddy o'Ryan's charming face creased by a broad grin.

"*That's* better! You'll have to be stirring, me dear! We're nearly into Basle and everything to put together! Rouse yourself, do! The time I've had trying to wake you!"

She let go of Kathie's shoulders and began to lift the cases down from the rack and pile them neatly together.

Then Biddy o'Ryan leaned out of the window, ready to summon the first available porter when they ran into the station. Dawn was breaking and a grey light turned the lamps pale and wan.

"Is this Switzerland?" Kathie asked.

"Just, we've to go through the Customs here before we do anything else and, whatever you may feel like, I want a wash and some hot coffee. Mind you have your passport ready. They'll want to see that, too."

The train clanked slowly alongside the platform and Biddy, seizing her cases, led the way out and down the steps where they were met by a young porter in a blue cotton smock and high, peaked cap, the uniform of the Swiss porter. He took the cases and they followed him to the Customs House where one official demanded to see their passports while another threw back the lids of the cases which Biddy had unlocked and ran his hands expertly down the sides and lifted a few of the contents. He nodded and slammed the lids down, chalking a cross on each with a nod to Biddy.

"Zist gut, Fräulein." He added a sentence or two in something that *sounded* German to Kathie, but was no German she had ever met before.

17

Miss o'Ryan laughed and tossed him back a quick answer as she locked the cases. Then, nodding to Kathie to pick up hers, she led the way to the Station restaurant where they sat down at a little table and Biddy ordered Gipfeln and coffee.

"What was it you talked to the Customs man?" Kathie asked curiously as they waited for the trim waitress to bring their order.

"Schwyzerdutsch," Biddy said. "It's the Swiss tongue that's spoken here in the north. In the south, you get Romansche. I suppose you'd be calling it a dialect, really. Anyhow, it's as well to have a little, for at least seventy per cent. of the Swiss speak it. Here comes our breakfast. Can you eat black cherry jam at half-past six in the morning?"

"Jam like that at any time!" Kathie assured her with an eye to the rich conserve placed before them with pats of golden butter and a piled-up plate of horse-shoe rolls.

"Well, make a good meal. We won't have our elevenses before half-past ten, for we can't spend too much time on the road. Stoke up!" And Biddy pushed over the plate.

Kathie obeyed her. The snap in the air made her feel hungry. Besides the jam lived up to its appearance and by the time she and Biddy had finished. the plate was empty and both felt much better. Kathie had shaken the last of the sleepiness from her eyes and was ready for anything.

"We'll have a wash and brush-up," Miss o'Ryan ordained as they left the restaurant. "If we had time, you could have had a bath." She stopped there, eyeing her companion with hopeful eyes.

Kathie rose at once. "A *bath*! At a railway station?"

"Oh, yes; they have bathrooms here for the use of travellers. However, I think you'll have to wait till we get to the Platz. We'll make do with a good wash. The water's always boiling."

Twenty minutes later, washed, brushed. and feeling several shades cleaner, Kathie followed Biddy out of the Bahnhof into the Bahnhofplatz with its fountain and flower beds, still gay with flowers. In the centre stood the Tramhüsli or tram station on which the tram lines converged from all directions.

"You don't get many buses in Switzerland," Biddy explained, "but the trams go quite a rate. No; we won't take one. Our garage is quite close, so it isn't worth while. We'll just walk there."

"What crowds of people for so early!" Kathie exclaimed as they left the Bahnhofplatz and swung out into a broad street down which men, women and children were streaming along.

"Work begins early here," Biddy explained. "Shops and offices open at eight and, except in the winter, schools at half-past seven. Work goes on till noon then there's a two-hour break for Mittagessen. Then work again until four o'clock for the schools and six for the grown-ups. Oh, by the way, I may as well warn you that here, we use Middle Europe time."

"What's the difference?" Kathie asked in puzzled tones.

"Well, instead of stopping at twelve and going back to one—two—three, they just go straight on, thirteen—fourteen—fifteen—right up to twenty-four."

"Heavens!" Kathie was horrified. "At that rate, I'll never know where I am after about four o'clock. Do we do it at school?"

"Oh, yes. Don't look so aghast. Sure, you'll soon get into the way of it," Biddy consoled her. "And here we are at the garage. Now where are those two girls?"

As if in answer, a slim, very trim person suddenly appeared from the little office to the garage and Biddy ran forward.

"There you are! Did you have a good time? Where's Sharlie, the creature?"

"Here!" And a girl of Kathie's own age appeared from behind the other. "What an age you've been, Biddy! We've been waiting here twenty minutes."

"We had to have a wash. You know yourself what the trains are like. Miss Ferrars," Biddy turned to Kathie who was standing shyly to one side, "this is Miss Burnett who is our games mistress and an Old Girl like me. This other one is Miss Andrews—*not* an Old Girl. The new mistress for Intermediate Fifth, you two. Sharlie, I rather think you've lost your place as Staff baby. Miss Ferrars has just finished her university course."

"Yes; but hers would be a three-year course and mine was only two," Miss Andrews said as she smiled at Kathie. "I'm twenty-two now."

"So am I," Kathie replied promptly.

Miss o'Ryan turned to the man who had been standing

waiting till they finished their chatter. A few remarks and presently he departed and returned, driving a smart runabout with the cases of the other two already strapped on to the luggage carrier. He seized on the other two suitcases and set to work to deal with them while Biddy ordered the two youngest into the back of the car and Miss Burnett into the front seat beside her. She paid the garage fees and scrambled into the driving seat. The man shut the doors and a moment later they were swinging into the stream of traffic which was already pretty long.

It took some time for them to clear the main streets, though Biddy o'Ryan was a clever driver and knew short cuts. At last, however, they were clear of the main traffic stream and driving through the suburbs where things were a little quieter. As they passed the end of one road, she half-turned and nodded towards it.

"Down there is where the Old Girl these two have spent the night with lives. You'll be meeting her sooner or later. She's one of the foundation stones of the school, to quote Joey—I mean Mrs. Maynard. Those two have always been chums. Frau von Ahlen is a dear and always was. How are they all, Peggy?" She turned to Miss Burnett.

"Very well. Even Gretchen seems to be pulling up now. Frieda says their doctor is very satisfied with her and she's certainly begun to put on a little weight."

"Good! Poor Frieda! They've had a tough time with Gretchen! And how are Arda and Marie?"

"Quite well, too. Marie's engaged, but the wedding won't come off for another year. Oh, and Arda is talking of sending Roosje to the school as soon as we start a younger class. She nearly collapsed when she heard about Joey's ninth. She said she found three quite enough for her! By the way, Biddy, haven't you spent part of the summer at the Platz?"

"Yes; I came back from England with Joey and Co.— you know they had to go to see what was going to happen to Plas Gwyn now the Howells don't want it any longer. I saw them safely home and then went back to spend a few days with Madame in the new house before term began again. Oh, they're all very fit. Joey got rid of the boys last Thursday and Mike was going down to Montreux yesterday. Oh, didn't you know?" as both Miss Burnett and Miss Andrews exclaimed. "Winnie Embury has found a tutor for Robin and Paul and she suggested that Mike should go to them during the week to share him. Joey won't send him with Steve and Charles until he's seven and the twins are too young for companions for him and he's never out of mischief as a result. Joey simply leapt at the idea. I think," she added pensively "that she has a new book simmering. Anyhow, Mike will go down from Mondays to Fridays and spend the week-ends at home. And, of course, he's fairly handy if Joey wants to see him apart from the week-ends, so it's a good arrangement all round."

"What will happen when the snow comes?" Miss Andrews asked.

"I wouldn't be knowing. Winnie may keep him at Montreux for the rest of the term. At any rate he's settled till that happens, which is something. Joey's clamouring for us to start a Kindergarten. Her twins will be ready for it in another year or so. Then there's Hilary Graves' girl and the boy the Peters have. Oh, and here's news for you. There's a new doctor arrived at the San—Dr. Morris. He's married and they have two girls and a boy as well as a baby of a year. The girls are five and the boy's three. We'll have quite a good start for a baby form by next September and I think the Head's considering it seriously. If we do have it, Winnie would send her two."

"But won't Robin be going with the rest to prep school? Miss Burnett asked.

"Yes; but there's young Alan coming along. Joey says that by the time next September comes, there'll probably be a dozen at least. However, it's all very much in the air at present. Now we're coming into the autobahn and I must give my mind to my driving, so talk to Miss Ferrars instead of me. you two."

She refused to talk after that and Miss Burnett, after pointing out one or two objects of interest to the newcomer relapsed into silence, too, and Kathie and Miss Andrews were left to entertain each other.

"Is this your first job?" Miss Andrews asked shyly.

"Yes," Kathie responded equally shyly.

"You'll like it here." Sharlie Andrews was sure about that. "It's a wizard school and everyone's so friendly. You must let me know if I can help you at any time and I will. I could tell you things and show you where things are kept."

"Oh, thank you. That would be awfully decent of you," Kathie said.

"What are your subjects?" Mis Andrews persevered, while Biddy projected a secret grin at Peggy Burnett over this prim conversation.

"Maths and geography. And I believe I'm to take some English subjects with my own form as well. What do you take?"

"Oh, I teach the Thirds. They're a jolly crowd—mostly ten-year-olds. As you've heard, we don't really take Juniors though it sounds rather as if we might begin next year. There's a big Junior School at Carnbach, of course. Most people, you see, don't fancy sending their girls abroad earlier than about thirteen or fourteen."

"I should have thought even that was awfully young," Kathie observed.

"It is, of course, but most of them are with us because they have people who are either ill or threatened with illness. It makes it easier and happier for them if they can have their girls close at hand. That's why health comes before everything else in the school. The girls get a lot of outdoor work and walks and scrambles whenever it's possible. We're tied a good deal to the house in the winter, but if we have fine weather, lessons more or less go to the wall and we're out. Of course, on shut-in days, we work double tides to make up; but you'll find that though we have a time-table, it's never rigid." Then she asked with real curiosity, "How about French and German? Can you speak fluently?"

Kathie was thawing under this shy friendliness. "I can speak them all right," she said, "but I don't think I'm frightfully good—not like Miss o'Ryan, for instance. When I heard her speaking French in Paris, I simply gasped. She just *was* French."

"Oh, well, she's been speaking ever since she was a small kid," Sharlie Andrews said quickly. "She was practically brought up by the school. She told me all about it one day last term. She was an orphan and the school adopted her as she had no one left to do it. Her home is with Mrs. Maynard in the holidays; but she says that it's really the school that's been home to her, ever since she was a kid."

"How awfully decent of them!" Kathie exclaimed.

"They're like that. It's an awfully *happy* school. We're

22

all friends. For instance, we all use Christian names."

Kathie nodded. "I noticed that you three all did. Do you mean everyone does."

"Oh, yes—out of school, of course. We're very proper when the girls are about." Miss Andrews laughed. "I was 'Sharlie' by the time I'd been here a fortnight."

"What is it short for?" Kathie asked curiously. "I've been wondering. It's a pretty name."

"I was christened 'Charlotte' and they called me that at my school. But at home, I've always been 'Sharlie' and so I am here. What's *your* name?"

"Kathleen—but they always call me 'Kathie' at home."

"I like that. May I call you Kathie?"

Kathie's eyes lit up. "Oh, *would* you? I've been feeling such an outsider, being 'Miss Ferrars' and all of the rest of you using Christian names."

"Of course I will. And you call me Sharlie. The rest will soon follow our example."

Miss o'Ryan and Miss Burnett had been carrying on a conversation of their own and paying no heed to their juniors, but now Biddy o'Ryan proved the truth of Miss Andrews' remark by saying as she swung into the long line of traffic heading through the suburbs of Berne towards the old town, "Miss Ferrars, do you want us to go on calling you that or do you like us to be using your Christian name? For I warn you, we're very much off our dignity out of school hours."

"I'd much rather fall into line with everyone else please." Kathie said.

"Good! Well, you'll be knowing ours; or if you don't 'tis deaf you must be. I'm Bridget or Biddy o'Ryan, very much at your service; and this is Peggy Burnett. The rest you'll be getting to know in time. And now, what's yours?"

"I'm Kathie."

"Kathleen or Katharine?" Peggy Burnett asked with a smile.

"Oh, Kathleen. It was my mother's name, you see, and as she died when I was born, my aunt and uncle said I must have it."

"And a good Irish name, too!" Biddy returned cheerfully. "Well, here we are in Berne. Sorry we haven't time to visit the bears, but you can come down one afternoon with Sharlie or someone else and enjoy them. Lots to see

23

in Berne, too. Now here we are and let's be seeing where our pâtisserie is. I want coffee and cream cakes, I tell ye, and nothing else will satisfy me! "

Chapter IV

The Very Beginning

"Do we go up there?" Kathie gazed upwards in dismay at the steep road winding up and up the mountainside from the plain and turned wide eyes on Biddy.

After the coffee and the cream cakes—of which she had eaten three!—at Berne, she and Peggy Burnett had changed places and now she was sitting beside the history mistress who had contrived, even while driving, to point out a good many landmarks and beauty spots as they went along. She had exclaimed with delight at the vivid blueness of Lake Thun along the northern shore of which the road took them to Interlaken—the city between the lakes—and the great peaks of the Alps soaring into the blue sky and the clear-cut reflections in the still waters of the lake had thrilled her.

In Interlaken, Biddy had insisted on driving them the full length of the Hoheweg to show the newcomer the Kursaal with its lovely gardens and great floral clock. She had paused at a certain point and Kathie had feasted her eyes on the austere loveliness of the Jungfrau with her bridal veil of glittering glacier slipping over one shoulder.

Now they had left the Hoheweg, driving down the autobahn which ran across the narrow plain and had reached the opening which led to the path to the Görnetz Platz. It looked like a fairly good road, mounting between high walls of rock on either hand; but though Kathie had driven both up and down some fairly steep roads in her time, she had never yet seen anything to approach this and a sudden thought flashed across her that if the brakes didn't hold they would all be dashed to death in an instant.

Going in bottom gear, the little car began to climb. Up and up she went, slowly but surely, while Kathie sat silent and apprehensive in her seat, wondering what would happen if they met anything coming down at one of the hairpin bends. The two in the back seat were laughing and joking as they climbed and Kathie wondered how on earth they could bear to do it! Then Biddy suddenly turned to her and said cheerfully as they rounded yet another bend, "Last lap! That up there is the Platz."

With heavings and clanking, the gallant little car negotiated a last incline that seemed practically perpendicular. She reached the top and they ran out on to a grassy shelf that ran right back for a mile or so to the higher slopes. A huge building with verandahs on which could be seen tall white beds stood a quarter of a mile from the path and Biddy nodded towards it.

"That's the big San. It's also one reason why the school's up here. We have quite a number of girls with relatives there. It's always been that way, ever since Tiernsee days. The school *began* first, but the San followed in about two years' time and ever since then the two have been run more or less in conjunction.

"What is there further up—where that train was going?" Kathie asked.

"The Rösleinalpe and Mahlhausen and one or two other places—all shelves like this," replied Sharlie from behind her. "This is the largest, though, and we have the post office for the district. Isn't the air gorgeous?" She sniffed loudly.

"It makes you feel awfully fresh and fit," Kathie agreed, following her example. "I say!" as she glanced across Biddy at the panorama opposite, "what marvellous mountains! And so near, too!"

"Only about twenty miles or so," Peggy Burnett said drily.

"Honestly? But they look quite near from here."

"That's the clear atmosphere. It makes distances awfully deceptive. But those mountains are every inch of twenty miles away," Peggy insisted.

Kathie looked with awe at the peaks rising above peaks in a long never-ending line like frozen waves, crested with white foam. "I never even imagined anything so wonderful! It's like a great sea of stormy waves!"

"Isn't it?" Biddy said as she swung across the grass from the road to a much narrower track which divided a little further on into two forks. Nodding at the farther one, she said, "That leads to Freudesheim, Joey Maynard's

25

place. This goes to the school. The two gardens join and Jack Maynard had a gate cut in the hedge so that we could get from one to the other as quickly as possible. You'll be finding out all about it in time," she added as she turned into a wide drive with lawns on either side. Broad borders, filled with autumn flowers, edged the lawns and in the centre of each was a great bed filled with roses, still flowering gaily.

"Do roses grow as high up as this?" Kathie exclaimed in surprise.

"They do; but before winter comes, they have to be done up in straw and sacking to protect them from the frost," Sharlie said with a reminiscent smile. "You never saw anything so funny in your life, Kathie! They look just like a bunch of old women in shawls and bonnets! The girls give up all one Saturday morning to it when the time comes. Each form has charge of one part of the garden and you never saw anything like the competition between them!"

"And here we are at last!" Biddy said as she pulled up before a widely-opened door. Peggy, be a gem and take her round to the garage for me, won't you? I've to take Kathie to the Heads, meself."

"Take your cases, then," Peggy said obligingly. "Are you so sure it'll be 'the Heads'? Bill may have gone back to her own abode." She turned to Kathie. "'Bill' is Miss Wilson, co-Head with Miss Annersley who's your own particular boss. When it was decided to open a finishing branch in the Alps, she came as Head of it. Then just this last year, St. Mildred's moved up here because Welsen, where it used to be, is shut in by pinewoods and too hot in the summer. Everyone used to go limp there, I believe, once the heat came. So Bill came back to us to a certain extent. She teaches all the Senior science and chemistry and heat, light and sound. Davida Armitage sees to the botany and hygiene, though."

"It was Miss Wilson who interviewed me," Kathie said, "I liked her a lot."

"You take that car round and let me be taking Kathie to the Heads—or Head," Biddy said.

Sharlie had already vanished with a last encouraging smile at her new friend and Biddy led Kathie across the wide entrance hall to a corridor that ran across the back and along it, to a short cross-passage.

"This place began life as a luxury hotel," she explained. "Hence this rabbit warren layout. The Head has her study, sitting-room and Rosalie Dene's office down here. Upstairs, there are three bedrooms and a bathroom and a private staircase. It's a real private suite. Miss Annersley sleeps up there and so does Rosalie. The third bedroom is kept for any unexpected visitors. That door's the office and the one opposite leads to the drawing-room. This is the study." She finished as they came to a door at the farther end. She tapped lightly, opened the door and drew Kathie in. "We've arrived!" she announced as she turned to close the door behind them. "I've brought her, safe and sound. Here she is!"

Almost too shy to speak, Kathie glanced round during this speech. She was in a fair-sized room, full of autumn sunshine, with two of the walls lined with books, a big, business-like desk set across one window and sundry chairs and a settee for the other furniture. Sitting at the desk was a tall, stately woman with well-cut face, gleaming brown hair inclined to wave naturally, and keen blue-grey eyes which had obviously not yet needed glasses. She wore a dress of sapphire-blue silky material with demure collar of embroidered muslin. One hand wore a seal-ring. The other was ringless. There was a great kindliness on her expression and Kathie felt at home with her at once.

Sitting to one side was the mistress who had interviewed her, very trig and trim in smart skirt and shirt-blouse and Kathie made a discovery. She had thought on that first memorable occasion that Miss Wilson's hair was white and, with her very black eyebrows and lashes, it had given her a poudré look. But now as she sat with the sun shining on the thick waves, it was to be seen that there was a good deal of copper mixed with the white and Kathie wondered what had happened to make it like that.

Miss Annersley gave the new mistress little time to feel shy or frightened. She stood up and held out her hand. "Welcome to the Oberland," she said in the beautiful voice which, Joey always declared, was one of her greatest assets, "I hope you mean to be very happy with us and learn to love the mountains as we do if you don't love them already. Biddy, run along to Rosalie. She wants to see you as soon as possible—there's some hitch about those history readers you wished for the Thirds and she

27

wants to get it settled as soon as possible. Come back in ten minutes' time for Miss Ferrars though."

"Oh, my goodness! And term almost on us!" Biddy wasted not a moment, but dived through a doorway opposite the desk and vanished, leaving Kathie to face the two Heads alone.

Not that she had any chance to feel shy even then, for Miss Wilson now came to shake hands and say, "So you're safely here! I wondered if Biddy would lose you before she got you to us. However, she seems to have kept her head. And what do you think of the Platz—so far as you've been able to see it?"

"Oh, Nell!" Miss Annersley protested, laughter in her voice, "do give her time! The poor girl hasn't had any chance to see a thing so far." She turned to Kathie. "We're all so pleased to have you here."

"Th-thank you," Kathie stammered. "I was delighted when I heard you'd accepted me."

"I hope you'll always feel like that," the Head said, smiling. "Now sit down, for I'm sure you're tired after the long journey. Have you ever lived among mountains before?"

Kathie smiled back. "I've never lived with *mountains*, but my home is in the Cotswolds. Of course, they're mere anthills beside these giants."

"I know the Cotswolds," Miss Wilson said. "They're puling infants beside the Alps, I admit; but then we haven't anything of great height in England."

"Haven't you been abroad before?" Miss Annersley asked.

"Only to France—to Normandy and Britany and they haven't any mountains."

"Then you've plenty to see," Miss Annersley said, with a glance at her co-Head. "You'll find enough to interest you, I'm sure. And we have a good many Swiss dishes so you'll have to play Robinson Crusoe with them as well. I hope you'll enjoy them as much as we all do."

"And I hope you like coffee," Miss Annersley added with dancing eyes, "for here we don't have afternoon tea at all. You won't miss that too much, I hope?"

"Hilda, you're alarming her!" Miss Wilson said severely. "My dear girl, don't look so stunned. We don't ask you to fast from lunch to supper-time. We mayn't have tea, but we do have Kaffee und Kuchen. And when

28

you go to spend the afternoon next door, Joey Maynard will almost certainly give you 'English tea', as she calls it."

"She says it helps to let strangers down lightly," Miss Annersley said. "Well, Biddy," as that young lady re-appeared, "have you managed to settle things?"

"Not yet. I'll have to be taking time this evening to choose something else," Biddy said ruefully. "I'd no idea those books had gone out of print."

"You can go through the catalogues after Kaffee und Kuchen," Miss Wilson said. "In the meantime, I think you'd better take Kathie—we *may* call you that unofficially mayn't we?—up to her room and let her tidy up. Mitta-gessen will be in three-quarters of an hour. You people were terribly *late* coming."

" 'Twas the train from Paris. We were held up outside Basle," Biddy explained.

"You *would* be! " Miss Wilson retorted. "Run along, both of you. We'll see you later—or Miss Annersley will. I'm having Mittagessen with you, but I must get back to my own quarters after that, and see what's been hap-pening before Staff meeting."

Biddy o'Ryan nodded and slipped a hand through Kathie's arm. "It's going to be a full term, I'm thinking. Come along, Kathie. You'll be glad of a wash."

She drew Kathie out and led her off to the other end of the house and up a narrow stairway to a similar cross-corridor where the Staff quarters were. Kathie found herself in possession of a charming little room on the second floor. It was small, but very dainty with divan bed in one corner, covered with a pink cover and pillows tucked into rose-spattered cushion-covers for the day. Pink rugs lay on the polished boards and the casement windows had rose-sprayed curtains swaying in the breeze. There was a comfortable wicker chair upholstered to match, and a couple of other chairs. Against one wall stood a bureau-dressing table and one corner had been curtained off for a hanging wardrobe. Biddy pointed out everything, explaining that she might have what pictures she liked so long as she hung them from the picture-rail. A light book-case facing the foot of the divan had a desk-top which folded up when not in use. There was a light over it and one in the centre of the room.

"Electric light up here! " Kathie exclaimed.

"Oh, yes. There's electric light everywhere in Switzerland. With so much water power, it's quite easy. You'll find lonely chalets and huts lacking most of the amenities of life, but they all have electricity," Biddy said. "Now I'll show you our bathroom and then I'll leave you to have a wash and brush-up while I make myself fit to be seen. Come along!"

She led Kathie to the end of the corridor where she showed a small, spotless bathroom which, she explained, the new mistress would share with herself and two others.

"So mind you stick to the baths time-table," she added, laughing. "You'll find yourself painfully unpopular with us if you don't!"

"Oh, I will!" Kathie protested.

"Good! Here are your towels in this drawer. Have you soap and things? Then I'll leave you to get on with it. I'll come for you presently and show you the Staffroom and so on, but there won't be much time for that till after the meeting."

And whistling like a blackbird, Biddy departed and Kathie was alone.

Her first action was to fling off her coat and cap, fill the basin with the cold velvety mountain water and give face and hands a good sluice. Then she went to her room and brushed out her thick hair and even found time to change from blouse and skirt into the light woollen dress she had brought with her. By the time Miss o'Ryan came tapping at her door, she looked fresh and trim, and that young woman eyed her appreciatively.

"What a pretty frock! It's too warm yet for skirts and blouses, isn't it? Come along. The first bell is just about to ring and I wouldn't be knowing about you, but 'tis famished *I* am!"

She led Kathie downstairs along a perfect maze of passages and into a long, narrow room with windows looking away to the west. Long tables ran down the room, bare at present. The big one across the top was laid, though, and Kathie looked with interest at the checked cloth, with its carefully laid covers and glasses in all sorts of shapes and colours—ruby, sapphire, emerald, topaz, amethyst and chrysoprase. The other members of the Staff were coming in in twos and threes, laughing and chatting gaily of the holiday doings as they took their seats. Kathie was placed between Biddy and a charming person who, she found, was Miss Derwent, the English mistress.

The strange dishes were attractive, too. First, a creamy soup, sprinkled with finely chopped green herbs; then veal done up in some kind of piquant sauce. A huge hollow bun stuffed with jam and cream followed, and after they had finished and Grace had been said, they all adjourned to the Staff sitting-room where they had such coffee as the new mistress had never tasted in her life before. She looked up ecstatically after her first sip and remarked to Sharlie Andrews who was sitting next her, "This is nectar! Do we get it *every* afternoon, or is it a special effort?"

Sharlie shook her head. "Karen is Tirolean by birth and her coffee is always like this. The Swiss are good, but Austrian coffee is really something!"

"Oh, it is!" Kathie sipped again and then Rosalie Dene, the school secretary and another Old Girl, as Kathie was to learn, arrived and came straight over to the newcomer to bid her welcome.

Remembering what she had heard from some of her friends about *their* first day in school, Kathie told herself that she was very lucky to be with such friendly people. The Staff sitting-room hummed with holiday gossip, but everyone was careful to include her when possible and she was never allowed to feel herself an outsider.

Presently, Miss Derwent suggested that they should make a move to the Staffroom where Staff meeting was to be held and Kathie found herself in another pleasant room. It was obviously meant for work. Every mistress had her own table and chair with hanging bookshelf above. There was a huge cupboard running from floor to ceiling in one corner and here she was given a shelf for her oddments. Meanwhile, some of the other mistresses were pushing the tables together to form one large one and setting chairs round it. Two armchairs stood side by side at the middle and Biddy, as she pushed Kathie into the nearest seat, explained that those were for the Heads.

"Rosalie sits next to take notes," the Irish mistress explained. "The rest of us sit where we like."

Mlle de Lachennais, head of the languages staff, came to sit on the other side and as she did so, made a laughing remark about the solemnity of it all in her own tongue. Kathie blushed as she replied. After the way Biddy spoke,

31

she felt sure that Mlle would be horrified at her accent. However, that little lady nodded at her.

"You speak fluently, ma chère," she said. "For the accent, that will come in time. "It is a matter of practice and of listening. Have no fear. You will soon speak as well as anyone."

Then the door opened and the two Heads came in and the meeting began in earnest. First of all, Miss Annersley gave out escort duties to those mistresses who had to be off that evening to meet girls in Paris at the Gare de l'Est. This, as Kathie had guessed, went to the old hands. Matron, who had come in after they began, claimed a couple of younger mistresses for help in her department and Sharlie Andrews and Kathie herself were earmarked by Miss Dene to unpack stationery and put it away in the stock-room. Miss Lawrence, Head of the music staff, said that she had still to finish her practice time-tables which would occupy her whole morning, but after that, she was at the disposal of anyone who needed her. Miss Burnett demanded assistance in setting the gymnasium to rights, and Frau Mieders, who took all domestic subjects, remarked plaintively that everything in her cupboards needed sorting out if the girls were to be able to start work on the Monday.

It was all arranged with any amount of chatter from everyone and Kathie wondered anew at the friendliness of the whole thing.

"Now," said Miss Wilson when the last detail had been settled, "we'd better go through the new girls. Nancy," she looked across at pretty, plump Miss Wilmot, "you have three—Joan Damer, Sylvia Thane and Beryl Wood. Beryl is a San contact. Keep an eye on her, though she is healthy enough. She has her medical certificate."

"Very well," Miss Wilmot agreed. "Any tendency to look out for?"

"None; only at that age and with her family's history, a little watchfulness would be a good thing." She turned to Kathie. "Miss Ferrars, we'll leave your lot alone for the moment, I think, seeing they're *all* new to you. Biddy, you have the lion's share as usual in Upper IV. You have ten. The only one I need mention is Tessa Wynne who comes to us with a reputation for practical joking. Keep your eyes open."

"Oh, goodness! As if Upper IV didn't always be

keeping you on your toes!" groaned Biddy at this. "Did we *have* to have her?"

"We did. She's the niece of a very Old Girl of the school. How many of you remember Juliet Carrick in Tirol?"

"I do," Biddy said. "But I thought she married some-one called Donal O'Hara?"

"So she did. Tessa is her sister's only girl. Kay Wynne became an invalid three or four years ago and Tessa seems to have been allowed to run wild with her brothers in consequence. Anyhow, she was getting so outrageous, that Juliet decided it must stop. I gather she descended on the Wynnes who live somewhere in the Welsh mountains, and after a lengthy session with Kay, finally persuaded her to trust her treasured daughter to us. Juliet came to see us herself a fortnight ago and as, in any case, there are twenty-six in Upper IVa, we decided to give Margot Maynard a chance to prove that her reformation is very real and put her up to Inter V. She's on trial there till half-term. If she does well, she stays there, Miss Ferrars—Kathie. If not, Biddy must have her again; but I hope and think it won't come to that."

"No question of it," Nancy Wilmot said. "Margot's a proud little monkey. She would hate to be demoted—"

"To be *what*?" Miss Annersley demanded, her eyes dancing as Nancy went pink.

"Put back again, then," the mistress returned with a fleeting grin. "*Must* we talk beautiful English, even at a Staff meeting? How unkind of you!"

"Anyhow, no one needs to worry," Miss Armitage put her oar in. "Margot will stay in Inter V if it kills her!"

"It won't come to that," Biddy said, seeing the alarmed look on Kathie's face. "When it comes to brains, Margot can make rings round the other two. It's steady work and concentration that's been *her* pitfall up to now."

"*And* original sin," Miss Moore mentioned with a chuckle.

"Sure, she's a reformed character these days," the history mistress said defensively. "What with her dip in Lucerne Easter term last year and Mary-Lou's accident last Christmas term, she really has pulled up. I don't say she's a budding angel or anything like that, but she does stop to think before she does mad things. Anyway, if I'm

33

B

to have a girl like Tessa Wynne, I'd be just as glad to have Margot elsewhere."

"She will be with cette méchante Emerence," Mlle reminded her.

"We can't hope to keep those two apart for ever," Miss Annersley said. "And Emerence has really begun to grow up since that same accident of Mary-Lou's."

"Well, Margot goes up," Miss Annersley said firmly. "Whether she *stays* up or not, will depend on herself alone. And now, we had better finish as soon as we can. It's half-past fifteen already and I'd like to remind you we haven't begun to deal with the lower forms yet."

The conversation ceased and she and Miss Wilson dealt with the remainder of the new girls before passing on to special duties, in the course of which Kathie found herself appointed Junior librarian.

"The prefects run the library," Miss Derwent, who was Senior librarian, explained later. "We see to the ordering of new books and overlook them and help in any difficulties they can't tackle. I'll hand over the fiction libraries to you and keep the reference myself. I don't know who you'll have for prefects—they settle that among themselves—but you'll find whoever they are will be very conscientious and eager to help. I'll give you a copy of the rules and your main worry will be to see that they are rigidly kept. If they're not, we shall soon run short of books. Girls are careless creatures. Oh, you'll have to discuss new books for the lists with them. You'll be given a certain sum and it's got to cover both Senior and Junior, so be just over your lists and as economical as you can."

This came later. In the meantime, the meeting finished and the Heads and Matron retired while the maids brought up Kaffee und Kuchen and the Staff relaxed.

"What are you doing after this?" Biddy asked Kathie.

"Sharlie said she'd take me for a walk," Kathie replied.

"Good! I'll be up to the eyes meself with those wretched Readers, but one evening I'll take you meself and show you my own pet walk. Abendessen at half-past nineteen. We don't change tonight, though, and Sharlie won't make you late in any case. After that, I'd advise you to unpack and get settled. Tomorrow will be hectic! I'm warning ye!" finished Biddy dramatically as she went to demand more coffee from Mlle who was pouring out.

Kathie laughed, but when bedtime came, she thought

34

that if tomorrow was more hectic than today had been, she didn't look like having any time at all for being home-sick as she had secretly dreaded. Then she rolled over in bed once more, shut her eyes and fell fast asleep. The first day was over.

Chapter V

INTERMEDIATE FIFTH

"THEN that is all just now, girls. Stand! Turn! "

Miss Lawrence, Head of the music staff at the Chalet School, twirled round on the music stool and struck a warning chord before she swung into one of Sousa's inspiriting marches and the girls turned and marched smartly out of Hall. The Juniors, some eighteen or so ten-year-olds, led the way and the rest followed, ending with the prefects. Those important young ladies sat at one side of the great däis which ran across the top of Hall, and Kathie, standing in her place between Sharlie Andrews and Biddy o'Ryan, looked at them with interest.

This was the first full day of school. Yesterday, Kathie had been kept busy unpacking the great parcels of stationery. There had been little time for the new mistress to learn anything about most of the girls, for when they had arrived and put away their hats and coats and changed into house shoes, they had all been summoned to Abendessen and after that, the majority of the girls had gone to bed. As it was well after half-past eight—or twenty-thirty, as they called it out here—this was hardly surprising. During the short Prayers which preceded bed, Kathie had noticed that some of the younger girls seemed half asleep already.

Neither had there been time for anything of the sort this morning. She herself had been summoned with Miss Andrews to finish the stationery while the school had its early morning walk after Frühstück and as her seat at the staff table was in the centre with her back to the room, she had not really been able to see the girls until they came together after Prayers to hear what the Head had to say.

She was very favourably impressed by them. They all
35

looked bright, happy and were trim and fresh in the well-cut school uniform of gentian-blue with cream blouses and the school ties of crimson and silver. She thought that the prefects looked as if they were well aware of their responsibilities—and she knew already from Miss Andrews' chatter that prefectship at the Chalet School meant a good deal, one way and another.

Miss Annersley waited until the Head Girl, Elinor Pennell, had tailed on at the very end. Then she turned with a smile to the newest member of the staff.

"And now, Miss Ferrars, come along and be introduced to your form with all due ceremony. I'm sorry the Maynards weren't in yesterday," she went on as she led the way off the däis and across the entrance hall. "As a general rule, they are up here for the last week of the holidays, at any rate; but this term, they stayed with one of our old girls who is a great friend of their mother's, and only came on with the rest of the school so that they could be company for Simone's Tessa. Did you notice her in Prayers, at all—a leggy young thing with two black pigtails and very dark eyes? We're always delighted when our granddaughters come to us," she went on, laughing, "and Simone was one of our first pupils."

"I think I saw her," Kathie said doubtfully. "She was standing between a little girl with a mass of fair curls and another with straight hair cut short with a fringe."

"That's the one," Miss Annersley nodded. "Ailie Russell, the fair child, is the youngest daughter of Lady Russell—our madame, as the girls all call her. Judy Willoughby is a younger sister of our Games prefect. Before we join the girls, I'd just like to remind you that this is a new form for us and rather in the nature of an experiment. I know Miss Wilson explained when she interviewed you, but I'd like to do it myself now. You have nineteen girls. Half-a-dozen are too advanced to remain in Upper IV, especially as we have only the one Upper IV this term, but are too young for Lower V proper. For instance, the Maynards are not thirteen until 5th November. Then there are some girls who are old enough but who need rather more groundwork before we plunge them into the work our Fifths do. And finally, there are seven new girls of whom I can say nothing as yet. No doubt you'll be able to tell me something about them before the term is very much older." She flashed a brilliant smile at the listening Kathie. "You'll find you can do no work this morning. They have to get all their stationery and textbooks and that takes a little time. Then Matron will be calling for them to unpack. As a matter of fact, apart from anything you may be able to do this afternoon, you won't do any lessons today. Tomorrow, they have brief lessons in all subjects so that they have preparation set. Next week we begin in earnest. But we always reckon to take these first two days for settling in and begin work on the Monday." She paused and looked at Kathie invitingly.

"It seems a good scheme as this is a boarding-school," Kathie said, seeing that some comment was expected from her. "Of course, I was at a day-school and we always began term on a Tuesday and pitched straight into work. I'll be glad of it, anyway, to get to know some of them," she added feelingly.

"Yes. Well, come along and meet them. Oh, and though we don't insist on the proper language for the day being spoken altogether until Monday, it is always well to start on it as far as you can. You feel quite happy about that, I hope?"

"I can manage all right," Kathie said. Suddenly she smiled. "I wouldn't have dared to take this job on if I hadn't been sure of that."

Miss Annersley laughed outright. "Don't worry, my dear. I'm sure you'll find you can cope quite well with your girls. Jo Scott is form prefect and Len Maynard is her second. They are helpful young people and you can rely on them if you must. Now we'll go and see what they are doing, shall we?"

She smiled again and secured Kathie's loyalty for the future. Then she slipped her hand through the new mistress's arm and walked her down to the end of the corridor to a door whence came the sound of eager chatter. Miss Annersley opened the door and ushered their form mistress in to Intermediate Fifth. The hubbub of voices ceased at once and the girls rose to their feet while a girl of about fourteen with mischievous blue eyes in a pleasantly cheeky face rushed forward to shut the door after them.

"Thank you, Heather," the Head said; and Kathie, looking at the girl, made an instant note of the name. This was *one* girl she would know in future.

Miss Annersley went to the mistress's table and gestured

37

slightly. "Sit down, girls! This is your form mistress, Miss Ferrars. Jo Scott!' "

"Yes, Miss Annersley?" A bright-faced girl of fifteen stood up.

"Tell Miss Ferrars anything she wants to know, please." She looked round with a smile. "All of you do what you can for her." Then she departed and Kathie was left alone to tackle her form for the first time.

Kathie drew a long breath as the door closed behind the Head. For a moment, she felt almost panic-stricken. She also felt as if the world were made up of *eyes* which fixed firmly on herself. Then she lifted her head with the funny little gesture which had made her uncle nickname her. "The Filly" in the past, and sat down at her table. On it lay the slim, paper-backed book in which the names of the nineteen girls before her were neatly printed in a long column. Well, at least she had no need to ask anyone what to do about *that*! She uncapped her fountain-pen and sat down to take register. As she called each name, she looked keenly at its owner, trying hard to impress some of the faces on her memory.

Some of them were easy—notably the Maynard triplets. They had the same features although Margot's colouring was reddy-gold, Len was chestnut and Con was dark. Apart from that, Len wore her hair in a tidy pigtail and Con's was cut in a deep fringe across her brows, while Margot's was merely bobbed and tied up at each side with blue ribbons. She knew Jo Scott, too, so that made four of her nineteen with whom she ought to have no difficulty. A shy-looking girl with two thick ropes of pigtails dangling to her waist replied to the name of Rosamund Lucy and she knew Heather Clayton of the wicked blue eyes and cheeky nose. The rest as she realised resignedly, she must leave to time. Then, halfway down the list, she came to Yseult Pertwee and stared at its owner. Yseult would certainly not be hard to remember. She was very pretty, but her main point was a mass of corn-coloured hair which, in defiance of the reigning fashions—and also of the rules, as the young mistress was to learn speedily—she wore parted in the centre and flowing unconfined by ribbon, plait or even clip over her shoulders and down her back.

Kathie looked at her doubtfully. Surely even the Chalet School didn't allow this kind of coiffure during work?

However, she hardly liked to say anything at the very beginning, so she merely marked the girl present and went on with the rest.

As soon as the last girl had been marked, Jo Scott stood up and asked leave to take the register to the office.

"Miss Dene likes to have them in as soon as possible," she explained.

"I see. Thank you, Jo." Miss Ferrars replied, handing it over. "Hurry back, please. We have a good deal to get through before Elevenses."

Jo went off and Kathie turned again to her form. "One of you,—you please, Len Maynard—tell me if you have a form stationery prefect," she said.

"Oh yes," Len replied readily. "We always vote for Stationery and Flowers and Tidiness; and our form mistress generally sees to the elections," she added helpfully. "Shall we do that now?"

"As soon as Jo returns," Miss Ferrars said. "Have you all pens? And paper of some sort. You'll only want three slips."

Everyone had her pen and most of them produced small notebooks from which they tore out sheets and provided themselves and the new girls with the three slips. By this time, Jo had returned and was sitting in her place.

"We'll begin with Stationery," Kathie said. "Write down the name of the girl you think most suited for the job, please. Then fold over your slips and someone—you, Heather—can collect them."

An objection came from the middle of the third row of desks. "Please," said Yseult Pertwee, "what are *we* who are new to do? We don't really know anyone yet."

"No, of course not. I'm afraid you'll have to stand down this time, Yseult. You people will be able to vote another time."

Yseult subsided and some of the girls glanced at each other. They had had two minor shocks. The worse was undoubtedly Yseult's calm air of self-possession. The other was the fact that the new mistress seemed to remember their names so well. If they had only known it, Kathie was quaking in case she made any silly mistakes there!

The voting proceeded peacefully. Eventually, Betty Landon was appointed as Stationery prefect; Rosamund Lilley was responsible for the flowers and tidiness went to Joan Baker, a big girl, who seemed rather older than

39

the others and who flushed and looked pleased when she heard her name called out. Kathie wondered at it. She also wondered what sort of a mother the girl had to waste money on having a schoolgirl's hair so elaborately "permed".

However, there was no time for wondering. It was already after half-past nine and the girls had to collect their stationery and textbooks. She invited volunteers to go with Betty to bring the stationery and was at once assailed by a forest of waving hands.

She suddenly relaxed and laughed and Inter V, as they came to be called, felt deeply relieved. Up to that moment, their new mistress had looked so very solemn and almost severe.

"You can't all go," Kathie reminded them. "Len Maynard, you may, and so may Rosamund and—" she paused and looked round, striving frantically to remember names. "Heather, you may go, and so may—Emerence Hope, isn't it?" She looked at a slight, fair girl who contrived to combine sharp features with a good deal of prettiness and was rewarded with a beaming smile and also a look of respect.

This was another thing to wonder about, but Kathie shoved it to the back of her mind, sent off the quartette to seek the stationery and then turned to the rest of her form to remark, "I shall soon know you all by name. Now while those four are away, Jo, can you tell me how you manage about your textbooks? Are they handed over in subject piles, or does each girl go for her own?"

"In subject piles," Jo said firmly. "Should I go along to stockroom and see if Miss Dene can take us now?"

"I think you might. And Jo! If she is too busy to take you now, ask her when you had better go. We can't have you running back and forwards all the morning."

Betty arrived with her arms piled high with scribblers and Heather followed, equally heavily laden, so the mistress turned her attention to seeing them given out.

Jo returned to say that Miss Dene would be ready for them in twenty minutes' time, so Kathie, struggling hard with her memory, chose six girls to go when the time came and then turned her attention to distributing small sheaves of paper to everyone. She learned from the girls that everyone in Middle and Junior schools used exercise

40

books, but the Seniors were honoured with loose-leaved files and file-paper for each subject.

"We each have twenty-four sheets of lined paper and twenty-four sheets of graph paper to begin with," Betty explained, having been well primed as to this by Mary-Lou Trelawney who had once been Head of the Middle School and still seemed to feel a certain responsibility for the girls over whom she had ruled. "After that, we have to give in our names on Mondays to the stationery prefect if we want any more. Oh, and we each start term with three new pencils and a rubber and if you want any more, it has to go on the list. Shall I bring the ink-cans and fill the inkwells, now?"

"Is this all the stationery you need?" Miss Ferrars asked cautiously as she glanced at Len Maynard who was giving out double sheets of blotting-paper.

"Er—no. There are still the vocab—I mean vocabulary books to get," Betty said. "I forgot them. Shall I go for them?"

"Yes; and Betty! Ask if you may have some small sheets of blank paper, will you? You'll need them for maps and diagrams in geography."

"We have geography books," Emerence explained, waving her hand at a pile she had just brought and dumped down on a nearby desk. "Shall I give them out?"

"Oh good!" Kathie picked up one and examined it. They were interleaved with lined sheets, plain sheets and tracing paper and were highly superior articles and she beamed as she remarked, "These are excellent—just what we need. Give them out, Emerence. I see Miss Dene has allowed two for each girl. You want one for physical geography and one for the rest. Then is that all when Betty brings the vocabulary books? All right. Joan, you and your band may go to the stockroom now for text-books. Be as quick as you can. Time is simply racing ahead and I'd like to have them all given out before Break."

Joan and the other five rose and departed and Kathie told the others to put away their stationery and leave their desks clear.

"It's awfully decent having locker desks," Len Maynard remarked as she opened hers.

"What did you have before?" Miss Ferrars asked curiously.

"Folders—and lockers at the side to keep our things in. And these are new, too."

"Yes; I hope you girls will remember that and not, spoil them by scribbling on them or trying your penknives on them," Kathie remarked warningly.

The girls giggled and one or two looked rather conscious. It was just as well for some of them that Kathie had reminded them. Emerence had already been planning a neat inscription on hers and she was not the only one.

"We can pin up our time-tables on the inside of the lids, though, can't we?" asked a leggy person whose twinkling eyes and tiptilted nose hinted at a very fair share of mischief.

"Yes, if that is allowed as I expect it is," Kathie agreed. "But don't keep on changing its position. There's no need and it damages the desk-lid."

By this time, Joan was back, laden with history books and the rest followed, each equally burdened, and everyone became very busy. Desk-lids were all up and the girls sorted out their books in the desks. Just as the bell rang for Break the last lid was closed and the girls sat back looking and feeling very virtuous.

"Yes; well we've finished that," Kathie said. "Now stand!" She gave them a word and they marched out to the Speisesaal to seek milk and biscuits and, once those had been consumed, to escape out of the garden where they gave tongue freely to their opinions of the new mistress.

Chapter VI

MORE EXPERIENCES FOR KATHIE

AFTER Break the summons came from Matron and Intermediate V scarcely paused long enough to ask to be excused before vanishing from their form room. Kathie was not surprised. Even the little she had seen of Matron —"Matey", as most folk seemed to call her—had left her greatly in awe of the little lady. She could quite well understand that the girls preferred to keep on the right side of her!

42

She stood at the window of her form room, looking out at the crags opposite which seemed so near though they were quite twenty miles away, and wondered what she had better do with herself for the next hour or so. At this stage of her career, Kathie lived in a state of apprehension lest she should put the wrong foot forward. It would pass, of course, as she got more experience; but just at present she was living at a strain and was edgy in consequence. However, she had not long to wonder for a prefect arrived with a message from Matron. Would Miss Ferrars please go and help to oversee the unpacking for her form as Miss Wilmot, who, as House mistress of Ste Thérèse, would have normally attended to it, was out of school at the moment.

"Oh, of course," she said, turning from the window. "I had no idea I should be needed or I'd have gone with the girls."

"It's Miss Wilmot's job really," Lala Winterton explained. "She's had to go down to Interlaken, though, because someone's made a mull of ordering our new log books—log tables, I mean," she added as she saw the bewilderment in the mistress's face. "Anyhow, they've sent all the wrong things and Miss Wilmot said she'd go herself and see to it and Miss Bertram's busy with Lower IVb, so Matron thought you wouldn't mind helping out. It needs everyone available," she went on as they reached the foot of the stairs. "Emerence and Heather and Francie are one person's work at any time, and when you have Margot Maynard added for good measure—" she left it at that and Kathie broke into laughter at all her sudden stop implied.

"That sounds as if she were an imp of imps," she said as they mounted the wide stairs to the top floor where the trunk- room was situated.

"No-o-o," Lala said consideringly. "I wouldn't say that, exactly. She's like Longfellow's little girl 'that had a little curl'. When she's good, Margo can be a young saint. When she's bad she's the absolute limit!'"

Kathie suddenly remembered that she was a mistress and that they were talking of her own form, so she merely nodded and thanked Lala who went off downstairs on her own lawful occasions while the mistress went into the trunk-room.

This was a long, narrow room, running right along

under the eaves of the house. Here, all trunks were brought up by the men and here they were stored according to forms, once they had been emptied. Already all the Upper forms' trunks had been put into place and Intermediate V were hard at it with theirs. Each girl shared with another one of the long light wicker trays on which clothes were carried down to the dormitories, and over each couple stood either a prefect or a Senior, checking up on inventories as their juniors unpacked. Matron, a short, wiry woman in the early fifties, very trim and crisp in her spotless print dress with snowy apron, collar and cuffs and "Angels' wings" cap, was very much in evidence, whisking from one pair to another with such a speed that she seemed to be everywhere at once. She looked up as the mistress entered and gave her a welcoming nod and smile.

"Here you are! Sorry to bother you, but Miss Wilmot has had to go down to Interlaken and I want a mistress in charge at Ste Thérèse's when the girls begin coming over. You might just take charge over here until they are ready and then go with your own House girls as soon as they've unpacked. Thanks! Now then, girls, are you all here?" She looked round sharply. "Whose trunk is that over there with no one?"

"It belongs to one of the new girls—someone called Yseult Pertwee. Miss Dene met us coming upstairs and cut her out and took her to the office," Jo Scott said.

At that moment, Yseult herself arrived, still with her fleece of golden curls flying round her flushed face. The rest noted with keen interest that she looked upset. Matron fixed the floating locks with an eagle eye and became rigid.

"Are you Yseult Pertwee?" she asked sharply. "Then has no one told you that you are not allowed to wear your hair loose here?"

Yseult went even redder. "Miss Dene has just informed me," she said in a clear, rather over-cultured voice.

"But did no one in your dormitory tell you this morning?" Matron persisted while one or two of the girls looked at each other significantly.

"I believe someone did mention it," Yseult admitted airily, "but I didn't pay any attention to her. It is by my mother's wish that I wear my hair in this style."

Matron's long upper lip seemed to lengthen appreciably,

44

and the rest of the girls stared at this new girl who dared to speak like that to her.

"Well, as she has sent you to the school I presume she wishes you to conform to the rules," she snapped. "Those rules say that no girl may wear her hair loose except on Saturday nights and special occasions. At all other times if it is not kept short it must be either plaited or tied back. Have you either hair ribbons or a slide? If not, come with me and I'll supply you. You can't go about looking like that, at any rate."

"Oh, why not?" Yseult protested. "I always wear it hanging loose. It's so much more picturesque and uncommon that way, don't you think?"

For a moment, Matron was stunned into silence by this. But no one had ever seen her at a loss for longer than that and she recovered almost at once.

"My dear girl, you haven't come to school to look 'picturesque', but to get a modicum of learning and as much common sense as possible. Now please don't try to argue with me any more, but come at once and get that untidy mop of yours tied back." She laid a hand on Yseult's shoulder and marched her forth and Yseult seemed to be suppressed enough for the time being to go without a murmur.

"Serves her jolly well right," remarked Emerence Hope aloud. "Prunella told her this morning to tie it back and she wouldn't listen."

"Oh, no! She prefers to go about looking like a perambulating haystack!" retorted Betty Landon. "It's more *picturesque*! I say, someone, aren't there three of those Pertwee girls coming this term? Anyone know if the other two are like Yseult?"

"You stop talking and go on with your work," interposed the prefect in charge of the pair. "Matey will have plenty to say to *you* if you aren't any further on when she comes back."

Thus recalled to their duties, they gave up Yseult's appearance for the time being and returned to their unpacking with a vim that told Miss Ferrars, at any rate, that Matron was a power all right. She remained where she was, keeping an eye on the girls nearest her, for she was not very sure just what her duties might be, apart from accompanying the girls to Ste Thérèse's when they were ready. The elder girls seemed to manage quite well

45

and the Intermediate V did not dally unduly over their task.

Her attention was drawn to a pair a little further away when the tall, slim girl with a head covered with short crisp curls suddenly said in clear, carrying tones, "Well, it certainly doesn't seem to be here."

"N-no, I don't seem to see it, Mary-Lou," Heather Clayton remarked meekly.

"But it's marked in the inventory," Mary-Lou objected. "It's your mother's writing, too. It *must* be here, Heather! Look through what you've unpacked already."

"It isn't on the tray," observed Heather's partner, Rosamund Lilley, pushing back the long black plaits that tumbled over her shoulders. "We haven't unpacked any winter coat but mine. Heather's doesn't seem to be here at all."

"Then it *must* still be in the trunk. No one's going to send a girl to school in Switzerland minus a winter coat *this* term!" Mary-Lou retorted. "Who packed for you, Heather? Not yourself, surely?"

"No, Mummy did it, but—well—er—I *did* take out a few things after she'd finished to shove in some oddments I'd forgotten I'd want," Heather acknowledged.

"But even if you took your winter coat out you couldn't possibly overlook a big thing like that," Mary-Lou expostulated.

"I seem to have done. It isn't here, anyway," Heather replied more meekly than ever. "There's nothing left in the trunk but some of my winter undies and books and shoes and so on. If you look, you'll see."

Mary-Lou bent to look and then stood up, apparently robbed of speech. But she recovered quickly. "You didn't bring it loose over your arm in train?"

"No. As a matter of fact I expect it's hanging in my wardrobe at home."

"*What?*"

"Well, you see, it's new and Mummy was very particular about packing it so that it wouldn't crease. When I took it and some other things out, I hung it up.

Kathie noted with interest that Heather sounded every bit as subdued as if she had been explaining to Matron herself. She glanced at Mary-Lou. The girl was tall and slim and she carried herself well. She was not exactly pretty but it was clear that by the time she was grown-up

46

she would be very good-looking with her clear colouring, thick fair curls and heavily-lashed eyes. She had a little unconscious air of authoritative dignity which struck the mistress as unusual in so young a girl.

"I see," Mary-Lou said. "In that case, that's where it most probably is. Now your mother will have all the bother and expense of packing and posting it. Really, Heather!"

Len Maynard next door had been listening. She had finished her own unpacking and was only waiting for her partner to finish hers. Con was given to mooning and was always slower than the rest of the Maynard family. Now she shoved her oar in.

"Hadn't Heather better go at once and ask leave to send a post-card tonight? I could finish her unpacking for her while she did it. Mine's done."

"Yes; I think she had better," Mary-Lou agreed. She looked round. "Go and ask Miss Ferrars if you may, Heather. And for goodness' sake try to remember that you're a Senior now and get over such kiddish tricks!"

It was about the most crushing thing she could have said. Heather's face was fierily red as she got up from her trunk and came across to Kathie to proffer her request.

"Please, Miss Ferrars," she said, "I—I seem to have left my winter coat at home. May I have leave to send a post-card about it at once?"

Kathie was in a quandary. She had no idea whether she could give the permission or not. However, Mary-Lou had kept half an eye on Heather and she came over to help.

"Could you let her, Miss Ferrars? Miss Wilmot isn't here to ask, but you *are* in Ste Thérèse's so you could give leave."

"Very well," Kathie said with much dignity. "You may write your card, Heather, and explain to your mother."

Heather murmured her thanks and left the room looking thoroughly crushed.

Matron returned a minute later, followed by a resentful-looking Yseult who, robbed of her picturesque floating locks, had turned into quite an ordinary looking school-girl. Kathie reflected that the two tails fastened back from her face with slides were not nearly so artistic as the flood of curls she had previously sported.

Margot Maynard, working nearby with her boon

companion, Emerence Hope, glanced at the new girl and then muttered to Emerence, "What a difference! Oh boy! And does she know it. She's as mad as hops over it!"

"You're telling me," her friend returned with a grin. "Well it serves her jolly well right. We all told her this morning in dormy and she wouldn't take the slightest notice, even of Prunella and *she's* dormy pree."

"*No!*" Margot sounded suitably horrified. She went on, "There are two more of them, but they won't matter. The little kid has bobbed hair and the middle one has hers cut in a page's bob—just above her shoulders and the ends turning under. Rather nifty, I thought it."

Kathie wondered if she ought to pull them up for slang but before she had made up her mind, Mary-Lou, who seemed to have caught the infection from Matron and to have ears and eyes for everything and everyone, called them sharply to order.

"That's enough slang, you two! I suppose you don't want to have to put the best part of your pocket money in the fines box this term?"

"Oh, bother her!" muttered Margot as the prefect went back to her own charges. "Mary-Lou's a lot too much on the spot! I didn't know she was listening."

"Nor me," Emerence owned. "Still, she's right, I suppose. Rules come into full swing on Monday and you know yourself if we get into the way of using certain words we'll get landed over them sooner or later. Best be safe rather than sorry."

Margot lifted shoes and slippers out of her trunk, scrabbled wildly after some odd pairs of shoe-laces and then stood up.

"I'm done! That's the lot, Thank goodness everyone knows Mother is fearfully fussy about the packing or we'd have had a pree on top of us, too. You done, Emmy?"

"Just!" Emerence laid a book down at the side of the tray and looked round. "Please, Matron, Margot and I have finished. May we take our things to our cubeys?"

"Everything there? But seeing who packed for you two, I needn't ask. Yes; you may. Mary-Lou, leave those two and go over to St. Agnes with those girls who have finished, will you?" She turned to Kathie. "And I think

48

the Ste Thérèse girls are all ready, Miss Ferrars, if you would take them across."

Kathie marshalled her little procession and marched them away to Ste Thérèse House. The trunk-room was in No Man's Land and belonged to the whole school, so everyone had to leave that part of the building before Matron could send for the next form.

Thanks to Matron's organisation, everything went well. The girls knew better than to lag behind the rest and by the time the bell rang for Mittagessen, the last Junior had been unpacked and her possessions tucked neatly away in their proper drawers. The trunks had been pushed to one side and later on the men would arrive to build them up into neat piles until they were wanted at the end of term.

Mittagessen was nearly over when the Head, who had been keeping up a general conversation round the staff table, suddenly touched the little electric bell that stood at her place and its sharp "pr-ring!" cut across the quiet buzz of chatter among the girls. At once everything fell silent and all eyes were turned to look at her as she rose to her feet.

"This is a beautiful day," she said. "After your rest period, you may all get ready for rambles. Blazers, stout shoes and berets, please. And don't forget to take your raincoats with you. Karen has been warned and she and the kitchen staff have been hard at it preparing parcels and flasks for you. Miss Dene has put up a list of forms and places and the form prefect may go and look at it before rest period so that you know where you're going. You must be back at school at half-past eighteen because it gets dark so quickly after that. Go straight upstairs to change when you come in. Your mistress and prefects will join you outside in the usual places. That is all. Grace, please! Stand!"

The girls rose swiftly but it was plain to everyone that they were rejoicing over this and Kathie was not surprised when she returned to the Speisesaal in quest of her handkerchief, to find them racing about, clearing away at top speed.

Mary-Lou, who was on duty today, saw her and smiled at her. "Oh, Miss Ferrars, Hilary Bennet and Vi and I are coming with you and Intermediate V this afternoon," she said, her clear voice ringing through the great room. "Miss

49

Dene has given us the Auberge walk and we'll introduce you to the echoes. You'll love them!''

For a moment, Kathie was inclined to respond in the same friendly manner. Then her aunt's words about remembering to keep her dignity flashed into her mind. She must remember that she was a mistress now and not just another prefect. She smiled quite pleasantly at Mary-Lou, but with just a touch of stiffness.

"That sounds very pleasant," she said. "I'm sure I shall enjoy it." Then she retrieved her handkerchief and left the room, leaving Mary-Lou to mutter to her bosom friend, Vi Lucy, "Am I snubbed or am I not?"

Kathie went upstairs to the staffroom where the rest were all having coffee. Sharlie Andrews was waiting for her with a cup of hot coffee and a comfortable chair. She greeted her friend delightedly, and Kathie settled down to coffee and gossip. If they had been alone, she would probably have mentioned the episode to the other girl and learned from her something of the friendly relations that existed between Staff and girls at the Chalet School. As it was, nothing could be done about it. It was a pity, of course, for Mary-Lou was just the sort of girl Kathie liked and being a friendly person herself, would have contrived to help the young mistress in a good many ways. As it was, they were to go very far apart before things changed and Kathie, having bought her experience as dearly as one usually does, settled in to become the kind of mistress the Chalet School prided itself on owning.

However, this was all in the future. By the time coffee was over, the half-hour rest period which was insisted on every day for the girls, came to an end and everyone had to hurry off to change and get ready for the various rambles.

"Put on stout shoes, Miss Ferrars," Miss Derwent warned her before they parted. "Oh, and has anyone told you to take your knapsack down with you? Don't forget it. You'll need it for your sandwiches and flask. And don't, whatever you do, forget to go to Matey's room for a First Aid kit. If you do, she'll come running after you with it. She never lets any of us go off for more than an ordinary walk without one, and I believe if she had her own way, she'd make us take one then."

Miss o'Ryan, standing near, laughed. "All the same, 'tis fortunate we do many a time, as you'll own," she said.

She turned to Kathie. "Who's your prefects?"

"Mary-Lou and there are two other girls as well," Kathie said.

"Ah! Then 'tis all right ye'll be. Mary-Lou knows her way about and she'll be able to keep ye to the right roads," Biddy said, deliberately broadening her brogue. "Not that 'tis very far wrong ye could go along the Auberge path. But ye can trust to her. Well, I'm to take Upper V off to the Rösleinalp, so I'll be off. See you later!" And she skimmed off, leaving Kathie wondering half-resentfully *why* everyone made such a fuss about this Mary-Lou. She went downstairs to find her flock waiting for her on the path outside the Splashery windows. Mary-Lou had left Len Maynard to tell her where to find them. She wondered what she had done to deserve the snub she had received in the Speisesaal and was not minded to risk another.

"I've got your parcel and flask, Miss Ferrars," Len called excitedly as the mistress appeared. "And we're waiting for you on the path. Oh, and I've brought a tin whistle and the twins' string of bells for the echoes, you know."

Kathie looked at the bright face and laughed. "This sounds most mysterious," she said gaily. "Well, I'll know all about it presently, I expect. In the meantime, come along. We won't waste any more time. Thank you for my tea, Len."

She tucked the package and the flask into her knapsack where the First Aid kit was already nestling and then led the way to the side door where she found her form waiting for her with Mary-Lou and two other Seniors in charge. The girls were in line and obviously eager to get off. Mary-Lou named Vi Lucy and Hilary Bennet to the mistress.

"What order would you like us to take?" she added politely.

"I think if you'll go to the head of the line—Miss o'Ryan tells me you know the way—and the other two stay at the end to see that no one lags behind, I'll walk about the middle," Kathie replied. "Are you all ready, girls? Then lead on, please."

They formed as she had said and Kathie found herself walking at a brisk pace beside Margot Maynard and Rosamund Lilley who were paired off, while Emerence

51

Hope was further up the long file, partnered by one of the new girls. Kathie noted that the others whom she had been warned were fireworks were equally neatly separated and Len herself was partnering Yseult Pertwee who had not lost her sulky look as she stalked along, swinging her two golden tails resentfully.

"There's something odd about that girl," the mistress thought as they streamed along the so-called high road, the girls laughing and talking quietly and she herself answering the chatter of Margot and Rosamund who kept pointing out local landmarks to her as they went.

"Oh, well," Kathie decided, even as Margot waved towards a pretty chalet and informed her that Nina Rutherford's people were living there at present and they themselves went ski-ing and tobogganing about the slopes behind, "she'll come out of it presently. No one could go on sulking on a day like this and with this gorgeous air. I won't take any notice of her, but just enjoy myself."

Chapter VII

THE STAFF HOLD A SESSION

KATHIE enjoyed her first ramble in the Alps. The girls were all that was friendly and pleasant and Mary-Lou remained carefully in the background, even when they reached the famous Auberge where everyone who knew united to exhibit the echoes to the new mistress.

She had had a word with her friends before they set off that afternoon, for she had been genuinely puzzled by Miss Ferrars's attitude in the Speisesaal.

"I don't know what I can have done to Miss Ferrars," she said seriously, "but she certainly snubbed me good and hard. You heard for yourself, Vi."

"I know." There was a very thoughtful look on Vi's charming face. "I thought it most uncalled for, for you really only showed a friendly interest."

Hilary Bennet chuckled. "I can guess. You were your usual self—that's all."

The other pair stared at her. Then Mary-Lou gave tongue.

"My usual self, indeed! What do you mean by that?

I was quite polite and—and friendly. I didn't say anything to upset her that *I* can see."

"Change 'friendly' to 'matey' and I rather think that'll be the answer," Hilary replied. Then she condescended to explain herself more clearly. "You see, Mary-Lou, you do always talk to everyone in much the same way. I mean you're friendly all the way down from the Abbess to the most junior Junior. We're all accustomed to you. We all know it means nothing. But Miss Ferrars is absolutely new. I can quite well see that she may have thought you were being—not cheeky; that doesn't cover it. I think—well, familiar is more like it."

"But I wasn't!" Mary-Lou exclaimed in shocked tones.

"Use your sense, girl! *We* know that. But I rather think I'm right and that's why she suddenly froze up—as a delicate hint to you that she wasn't taking anything like that from even a prefect. It's up to you to act on the hint."

Mary-Lou considered this. "Ye-es; I think I see what you mean. Goodness knows you folk have rubbed it well in that I do and say things no one else expects to get away with and I do. I don't seem to have done that this time, though. And, you know, it honestly isn't meant for cheek. I'd better keep in the background this afternoon and leave it to you two and the Inters to tell her things."

"You'll never do it!" Vi said with conviction.

"Oh, yes I will. I can remember not to talk but if I *do* talk, I'll never remember to use a totally different manner. So I'll keep quiet. When she speaks to me I'll answer, of course. I can't be *rude*. But I'll try not to volunteer information free gratis. So that's settled. Perhaps by the time she's been here a few weeks she may understand that I'm quite harmless. I hope so because, you know, I like what I've seen of her. I could like her quite a lot, given time and a chance."

As a result, Mary-Lou was distinctly *piano* where the mistress was concerned that afternoon. On her side, Kathie thought the girl had taken her hint and was prepared to be on quite good terms with her so long as she avoided the manner which the young mistress *had* thought verging on the familiar—Hilary had been quite right there. Unfortunately for them, Kathie had been at the sort of school where the girls and Staff had nothing to do with each other outside of school hours. Of the camaraderie

53

which existed between the two divisions at the Chalet School, she had not the faintest inkling. Her attitude was more or less right where her own form came in. Intermediary V contained a number of people who required no encouragement from anyone. But where the Sixth Forms and especially girls like Mary-Lou were concerned, it was needless. However, like most of us she had to learn the hard way, by experience.

On Friday they began lessons and went hard at it. The time-table proper did not begin till the Monday, but on the Friday every form was supposed to have a short half-hour lesson with each mistress who taught it, art, domestic science and music apart. The mistresses set preparation for the coming week and, in the upper forms, gave some sort of outline of the work to be done that term.

Kathie found her own form very uneven. The girls who had come from Upper IVa at the end of the previous term were mainly well-grounded, though she saw that Joan Baker hesitated frequently and Rosamund Lilley seemed not quite sure of some ground. Of the new girls two, Eve Hurrell and Charmian Spence were up to standard, but Pamela Jackson, Marguerite Woodley and Iris Wilmot were not; and Janet Kemp, a Scottish girl who had come because her mother was in the big Sanatorium at the other end of the Platz and very ill, was head and shoulders above most of them. As for Yseult Pertwee, it was soon plain that she was a good two years behind the rest and had been educated on lines that her own grandmother might have known, and Kathie was moved to wonder if she could possibly keep up with the others when work began in earnest.

It was this in her mind that sent her that evening to buttonhole Miss Dene after Abendessen and Prayers were over and the Staff were relaxing over coffee and biscuits in their own pretty sitting-room.

Kathie took her coffee from Mademoiselle de Lachennais the doyenne of the Staffroom and then made a bee-line for the school secretary who was sitting on the big settee. She looked up as the new Staff baby came up to her, coffee in hand and a worried look on her face.

"Come along and sit down. What's wrong? You look as if you had all the worries of the world on your shoulders," she said, smiling.

"Miss Dene, can you tell me what one does about a
54

girl who is definitely nowhere near the standard of the form?" Kathie asked.

Miss Dene smiled. "What girl in which form isn't up to standard in your subjects?" she inquired. "And, by the way, you may have noticed that off duty we're all on Christian names terms as a rule. I'm sure you know I'm Rosalie and I know you're Kathleen of course."

"Oh, *not* Kathleen! I'm always Kathie, please."

"Kathie, by all means," Miss Dene acquiesced cheerfully. "So that's settled."

Kathie said rather shyly. "I've felt such an awful outsider, being 'Miss' while all the rest of you use your names."

"Poor you!" Rosalie leaned forward and spoke solemnly. "You'll soon find out that the Chalet School is at least a very friendly place. And now, tell me what's wrong that you look so over-burdened."

"It's that new girl, Yseult Pertwee. She simply isn't anywhere near the standard of Intermediate V, you know, and I don't know what to do about it."

Rosalie Dene looked suddenly anxious. "Oh, my dear, *not* that girl."

"But why not?" Kathie asked, with wide eyes.

"Because for age alone she's in the very lowest form we can manage. She *ought* to be in Upper V, but she couldn't begin to touch their work. She's sixteen and a half and the average age of Inter V is fourteen years eight months, so as it is she's nearly two years older than the average. We can't possibly make a Middle of her!"

"N-no, I suppose not," Kathie agreed unwillingly, "All the same, she's miles behind the rest in both maths and geography and her spelling is *wild*. How on earth has she been brought up? She seems to know practically nothing."

"She has an artistic mother who writes very lush novels," Rosalie said solemnly, though her eyes were dancing. "She also has Ideas."

"What sort of ideas?" Kathie demanded involuntarily.

"'I told you she was artistic. Doesn't that explain everything? Besides, look at the names she wished on to those unfortunate girls of hers—Yseult—Véronique—Valencia! Can you believe it? Though I understand," she went on with preternatural gravity, 'that Véronique's little playmates are already addressing her as 'Ronny' and Valencia has already been shortened to 'Val'. But what can you do about 'Yseult'?"

"Well, you might make it 'Izzy'—but I don't see our picturesque Yseult agreeing to that!" Kathie retorted with a giggle.

"What's this about Yseult?" demanded Biddy o'Ryan who had overheard this in passing and now came to sit down beside them on the settee. "Shove up a bit, Kathie, and make room for a little 'un, will you? And while we're on the subject you might tell me if you think Yseult knows anything at all about history."

"So you're fed up with her, too?" Rosalie remarked. "Kathie's just been wailing to me about her lack of maths."

"You listen to me," Biddy interrupted. "Kathie can come in on geography later."

Rosalie sighed resignedly. "Very well; go ahead. What's wrong with her history?"

"Everything—and then some," Biddy returned, lapsing into slang. "Would you believe it, she's never in her life been taught to argue from cause to effect or vice versa, and she hasn't the least idea of taking the wide view on anything. So far as I can make out, 'tis English history she's done and that according to reigns. A king's a king; but a great social or political movement may spread over half-a-dozen reigns. Now will you look at this! I'm starting the Tudors with that form for the sake of their General Cert. But they're also doing Empire history and ye know yourself that ye can't just be tied down to one country, anyway. So when I went to set their prep, I told them to read the first three or four pages of their text books and come prepared to discuss the reasons for the rise of British trade during the first ten years of the period. I also told them that as this was the era of exploration we should be doing something about tracing the founding of the Empire in our Empire history and we'd be able to run the two together this term."

"Nice work," Rosalie commented. "Let me know when you want the paper for charts and so on in good time, please. It has to be cut to size, you know."

Biddy dismissed this with a wave of her hand. "I'll tell you. Meantime, I went on to a little detail of what we should be doing. After all, they are *Fifth* and it's as well that they should have some idea of what we're getting at.

Most of them were quite keen. That new girl—what's her name?—Janet Someone or other—she was especially keen and asked one or two quite sensible questions. So did Len Maynard, but I'd expect it of her, considering Joey's craze for history. Yseult just sat there like a dummy so I smiled at her and said, 'Well, Yseult, and haven't *you* any questions you want to ask'? She just looked at me and said, 'Oh, I don't think so. I don't understand the idea at all. History ought to be interesting, like the story of Drake playing bowls when the Spanish Armada was sailing up the Channel. But how can trade or exploration be interesting? And it's too much. We are only school-girls. Surely such work is only suitable for university students'?"

By this time, quite half the members of the staff room were gathered round, listening and at this statement, they went off into shrieks of laughter.

"Poor Biddy!" Mlle gasped between her trills. "How grieved I feel for you, chérie!"

"But what did you *do* to her?" asked Miss Moore who was Kathie's immediate superior for geography.

"Nothing; though I could cheerfully have shaken the life out of her," Biddy said more calmly. "I simply told her that she'd be finding she had worse things than that to tackle before she'd finished with school and if she used her brains, her books and the notes I'd be giving them, she'd find 'twas easy enough."

"Did she seem to find any comfort in that?" queried Miss Wilmot, the senior maths mistress. She glanced at Kathie. "I'm sorry for you, my dear, if this is a specimen of *all* her work."

"I'm sorry for myself," Kathie said ruefully.

"What about her geography? Or don't you know yet?" Miss Moore asked.

"Oh, I know enough. She knows the countries and their capitals and I *will* say she seems to have learnt all her definitions. The snag is that so far as I can see she hasn't a clue how to apply them. They're to do world products and populations and that sort of thing this term with Africa in detail. They're awfully lucky—got decent atlases; and those synthetic maps they have are the last word. I gave out the Africas and told them to spend their prep time finding out how configuration tended to affect population. Some of them didn't seem to be very sure

57

how to manage, so I used the climate and production maps with the same idea. Practically everyone jumped to it almost at once and I left them going hard at it, testing one map against another. They simply loved it! But Yseult simply sat there and whether she took in a tenth of what I was saying is more than I can tell you. I shouldn't think so, judging by her expression."

Rosalie looked very troubled. "It's a problem, isn't it? I'll seize the first moment I can to put it before the Head. But one thing is certain. No matter how bad her work is, she can't be sent down to Middle school—not at sixteen and a half. So get that right out of your heads."

"That means intensive coaching," Biddy grumbled, "and I've plenty to do with my free time without taking on an ignoramus like that."

"I'll see what the Head has to say," Rosalie said. "I know when we looked over her entry papers she did make some remark about the child seeming to have learned nothing; but we took her and the other two because, though *they* know nothing about it and are not to know, their mother has to go into hospital for treatment and it's going to be a long job. That's why she sent them over here, right away from everything. They have no father—he was killed in a motor accident when Valencia was only two—and neither uncles nor aunts nor grandparents. You know what the Head and Bill and Madame are. They said all three must come here and we must do the best we could for them." Then she added, "there's no knowing what may happen about Mrs. Pertwee. They won't be poor; I know that. But if—well, if she shouldn't come through, they don't seem to have a relation in the world but some distant cousins who live in the States and whom even she has never met. It's a pretty poor look-out for them, poor kids!"

Kathie, with a sudden thankful remembrance of the happy home she had with the Graysons, felt that even if it meant giving up some of her free time, the least she could do would be to take on some of the coaching that Yseult must certainly have if she were to be at all able to keep up with Intermediate V.

"What about the other two?" Miss Wilmot asked.

"Quite bright on the whole," Biddy said. "Oh, the same dear old yarns, of course; but they were interested in what I said about their work and the second one—Ronny, I

58

heard some of that crowd calling her—asked one or two quite good questions. I think they'll manage all right. But Yseult is quite another cup of tea. Oh, well, if we must coach, we must coach, I suppose. But it won't be a treat for anyone, I'm telling ye."

"Well, you give school a miss now and come and have a game of Rummy," Miss Derwent proposed. "We get quite enough of it during the daytime without using up our precious evenings talking shop. Come along, everyone! I've got the cards and a sheet of paper to keep score and we've just nice time for a round before we ought to go to bed."

Everyone *had* had enough of shop. They settled round the table and in the excitement of trying to come out with a reasonably low score, Kathie forgot her worries and Yseult and went to bed to sleep soundly until the rising-bell next morning.

Chapter VIII

A Spot of Preparation!

Miss Annersley the next day said that Yseult was to have intensive coaching until further notice. The Head sent for Yscult and presented her with a new time-table and had what Blossom Willoughby, the Games prefect, called "a heart-to-heart" with her.

Yseult emerged from that talk feeling slightly dazed. One thing had been well rammed home, however: that in this school, she was expected to work and to work hard during actual school hours. It was at subjects such as arithmetic, essay-writing, geography and history that she was expected to work hardest. This came as a horrid shock. After more than three weeks of school, she had grown rather more resigned to confined locks; but to have to give up her easy efforts at work was something else again. And the Head, noting the way she slouched, added insult to injury by adding remedial exercises to the time-table. Truly Yseult felt that life was being very hard just now!

The immediate effect was a lengthy fit of the sulks.

59

The people who had her for coaching reported to each other that she was most unco-operative. That the mistresses had had to give up part of their free periods to do it never dawned on her and it is doubtful if she would have cared if it had.

By this time, Kathie had learnt that the prefects were mainly responsible for evening preparation. Friday night was an exception. Then, they had a special literature lecture from the Head so she and Miss Andrews took it in turns to take duty in Hall with the entire Middle School. Mlle Lenoir, the youngest of the music staff, had the Juniors and Miss Bertram took charge of Intermediate V. There were too many firebrands in that form for anyone to trust them to work completely alone for two hours on end! Once in three weeks, she was relieved by whichever of the other two happened to be free.

On the fourth Friday of that term Kathie had just settled down comfortably in the Staffroom when she was summoned to Matron.

Matron said briskly. "I want you to take Miss Bertram's prep with your own form this evening, please. Joan Bertram hasn't been feeling very well this last day or two and when she was going downstairs to take prep, she suddenly turned very faint. Luckily, Elinor Pennell was just behind her and saw her sway and caught her just in time or she would have gone headlong down the stairs. It's just one of her usual bilious attacks and I've sent her to bed where she stays till it's over. In the meantime, she's worrying about your form's prep. If you'll take it, I'll see Rosalie Dene about her actual lessons and she'll tell you what she's arranged."

With an eye to the time, Kathie bolted back to the Staffroom to gather up her maps and broadcast the news before she went down to her form room.

Kathie scrabbled for her red ink Biro and looked round to see that she had all she would need.

"Better take a cardigan with you," Nancy Wilmot advised as she drew her pen across an entire sheet produced by Verity Carey of Upper V. "There's a nasty draught in that room of yours—I noticed it last year, but I don't suppose anyone bothered to report it as we only used it for emergencies then. I'll report it to Frau Mieders tomorrow, since she sees to all that sort of thing. In the

meantime, if you don't want a chill, take precautions!"
She looked over the remainder of Verity's work and
moaned loudly. "Does young Verity ever even *try* to
reason? I wish she'd stop maths, for she doesn't seem to
know what she's doing more than half the time."

"I know," observed Miss Armitage, who took botany
and Junior science. "I flung her out of my botany classes
last year—told the Head it was sheer waste of time for
her to go on. Why don't you do the same, Nancy?"

Kathie heard no more for she had left the room and
was racing downstairs. She felt that the sooner she was
with her form the better. Most of them could be relied
on to behave themselves, but with people like Emerence,
Margot, Heather and Francie, she had already learned
that it was well not to be too trusting on all occasions!

As she neared the door, she heard a clear voice saying
sharply, "Now that's quite enough, Francie! Rudeness
won't get you anywhere. You've disturbed Miss Annersley's lecture so that she had to send me to tell you to be
quiet as if you were a set of Third form babies. You'll
hear all about it later, I don't doubt. Don't make things
worse for yourself. Get down to your work and stop being
such a silly little ninny!"

With a feeling of dismay, Kathie pushed open the door
which was partly ajar and marched into the room
Mary-Lou was there, standing by the table, and Francie
Wilford, looking decidedly mutinous, was standing up in
her place.

"What is wrong here?" she demanded, while the form
leapt to its feet and Francie went suddenly red. "Why
are you here, Mary-Lou? And what had Francie been
saying that is rude?"

Mary-Lou flushed slightly. "The Head sent me to tell
them to be quiet, Miss Ferrars. Francie was just a little
rude to me over it. I was only staying until someone came.
That's all." She spoke nervously, for the weeks that had
passed had not made matters any better between them.

"I see. Well, I'm here now so you may go back to your
lecture. I'll see the Head later and apologise to her.
Thank you for taking charge." For the life of her, Kathie
could not help a chilly tone creeping into her voice.

Mary-Lou turned to go, but Kathie called her back.
"Oh, just a moment, Mary-Lou. Francie, apologise at

once for being rude to a prefect—especially one sent to you by the Head."

Even the back of Francie's neck was crimson as she mumbled her apology under the cold glance of the mistress. Mary-Lou accepted it and then left the room and the young mistress faced her dismayed form.

"I'm ashamed of you!" she said severely. "Just because someone doesn't come to take charge of you as soon as prep begins, you actually behave so badly that you upset Miss Annersley's lecture and have to have a prefect sent to take charge of you as if you were a set of Juniors! No, Jo!" as Jo Scott opened her lips. "I don't want to hear any excuses now, thank you. Sit down, all of you, and go on with your work at once. You've already wasted a good twenty minutes of the time, so you may make it up later on. You will all come back here after Prayers and work for twenty minutes then. Now begin at once, please!"

The girls sat down in silence and set to work while she arranged her table to suit herself. She knew that, annoyed as she was with the form for such bad conduct, it was finding Mary-Lou of all people there that made her so really angry. She knew that she was being foolish and prejudiced, but her fear lest she might lose her dignity and the memory of her aunt's words on the subject made it hard for her to alter her attitude as yet. This made things worse, for she was also vexed with herself for what she recognised as an unreasonable frame of mind. She settled down to her maps and went on with them, frequently looking up to see that the girls were working and not playing.

At first, all went well. The form had a full evening's work before them and those people who had no part in the trouble buried themselves in it and the rest followed their example. But Francie had a queer temper. Mary-Lou had scarified her thoroughly before Miss Ferrars arrived and she had the prospect before her of hearing the Head on the subject later on. Kathie's added remarks had roused the devil in her and she was only waiting until the mistress became absorbed in her own work.

She scrambled through her arithmetic and then took up her history. It was very annoying that Friday should be a "French" day and not only were the questions posed in that delightful language, but they must also be answered

in it. Francie always found that this added half as much
again to her labours.

Having dealt with her history, Francie turned to her
worst bugbear—free French composition. Even in English,
she rarely produced more than the baldest kind of essay.
To have to write one directly into another language always
floored her. Tonight when she was badly upset to start
with, she found it even harder than usual. She produced
three sentences on "Le Livre lequel j'aime le mieux" and
then gave it up.

After sucking the end of her pen, wriggling until she
nearly overturned her desk and drew on herself a reprov-
ing look from the girl immediately in front of her, and
generally making a nuisance of herself, Francie peeped
at Miss Ferrars through her long lashes. Kathie was
frowning over a map of Isabel Drew's and seemed to be
fully occupied. Francie stealthily tore a strip from a page
in her scribbler, rolled it into a tight pellet and looked
round for a victim. In the row in front, a few seats to the
right, Len Maynard was scribbling industriously at her
history. French had no terrors for *her*. The sight of her
absorption put the finishing touch to Francie's bad mood.
She took deliberate aim and flung the pellet hard at her,
hitting her on the nose.

Len dropped her pen with a start and a smothered
squeal, for the blow had stung. Miss Ferrars looked up
instantly and her face was very black.

"Who made that noise?" she asked sharply.

Len stood up, red to the tips of her ears. "I did, Miss
Ferrars."

"And why, may I ask?" There was a nasty edge to the
mistress's tone.

Len had a very good idea who had flung the pellet, but
she was telling no tales.

She stood in her place, her round cheeks very pink and
her eyes on her desk. Emerence, who had seen the whole
thing from her place at Francie's left, darted an accusing
look at her, but Francie set her teeth and said nothing.
Let that little prig of a Len get into a row if she liked! It
would do her good!

If she had been her normal self, the girl would have
known that if she did not speak, someone else would. She
would also have known that it would mean bad trouble
for herself with the others, but just at present she didn't

care. She sat sucking the end of her pencil and gazing nonchalantly into space.

"I asked you a question," Kathie reminded Len when the silence had lasted a full minute. "Why did you make that noise?"

"I—I—" Len stammered; and got no further.

Kathie waited another minute. "Come out here," she said at last.

Len marched up to the front of the room and stood facing the mistress.

"Now," said Kathie, fully roused by this time, "you stand there until you choose to answer my question. I shall watch the time and you can stay on when the rest go later and make up for what you have wasted then."

She turned back to her work and Len stood there, very red and angry. She was generally the sweetest tempered of all the Maynards but, as her mother had once remarked, she didn't have red hair for nothing and now she was furious. She wasn't going to tell any tales, but just let young Francie—she guessed who had done it—wait until they were free! She'd hear all about it then!

However, if Len refused to tell tales, Emerence had no such inhibitions. She stood up. "Please, Miss Ferrars!"

"Well? What is it?" Kathie asked, still sharply.

"It wasn't Len's fault that she squalled out. Someone threw a pellet at her and hit her on the nose. I saw her do it."

Kathie laid down her Biro. "I see. Len, do you know who did it?"

"No, Miss Ferrars." Len replied, thankfully reflecting that this was the truth. She did *not* know; she only suspected.

"I see. Very well. You may go and sit down. And," Kathie was determined to do things thoroughly, "I beg your pardon for scolding you."

Redder than ever, Len went back to her seat and sat down thankfully. Kathie brought the rest to attention.

"Girls! Put down your work!"

The form came to attention instantly. There was something in their mistress's tone that warned them that she was not to be trifled with.

"Who threw that pellet?"

Faced by a direct question, Francie decided that she had better own up. But the look she cast at Emerence as she slowly got to her feet was the reverse of amiable. "I did it, Miss Ferrars."

"And then left Len to bear the blame?" Kathie said in her most scathing tones.

Francie said nothing. She looked down and fidgetted with her hands.

"Stand still! And look at me, if you please!" The command rang out like the crack of a whip and the girls jumped. So far, they had seen only the pleasant side of their mistress. They had no idea she could be like this.

Francie looked up apprehensively. What she saw sent her eyes down again.

Kathie glared at her and then turned to the others. "Go on with your work, the rest of you. Frances!"

The unlucky Francie flinched at the unaccustomed sound of her full name. "You may stay there for the rest of preparation. Perhaps that will teach you to bear the blame for your own sins in future."

At this awful retribution, Francie began to babble wildly. "But, please, Miss Ferrars, please, I haven't done anything hardly—only my arithmetic and history and—"

"You should have thought of that before you started trying to upset other people," Kathie said inexorably.

"But—but——"

"That will do. I have told you what you are to do and I don't wish to hear anything more from you. You will come back with the rest after Prayers and stay until you have made up your full preparation time."

Francie subsided miserably. This meant that she would be doing prep till nearly bedtime. Furthermore, as she very well knew, she couldn't hope to finish her work because so much time had been already wasted. *That* meant that while the others would be free after the first hour or so of the morning's school to do their home letters or read their library books, she would have to work. As for Emerence Hope, she was a nasty-minded sneak, getting other people into trouble like that—Francie conveniently forgot that she had left Len to bear the blame for her misdeeds—and she would pay her out sooner or later She gave Emerence a baleful glare but as that young woman was struggling valiantly with her French essay, it was wasted for she never saw it.

Kathie went back to her correcting, but she was unable to go on comfortably. Intermediate V had been thoroughly

65

C

upset and the girls were restless. Pencils and rubbers were dropped; someone upset the pile of books at the side of her desk and looked literally scared when called to order. As a crown to the evening, Yseult, who had just come in from a coaching in history with Miss o'Ryan, did little but fidget with her belongings. She certainly did no work.

Kathie kept a wary eye on them all and presently she addressed Yseult. "Have you finished all your work, Yseult?"

"No," Yseult replied at her airiest. "I can't do much of it, I'm afraid."

"And *I'm* afraid you must try—or come to me for extra coaching tomorrow afternoon."

Yseult had been lounging in her seat, but at this bland remark, she shot upright.

"Eh?" she said in stupified tones.

Kathie repeated her statement and then added, "And we don't say 'Eh?' if we have not heard clearly what was said to us. It is considered better manners to say 'I beg your pardon'." She spoke in French, of course, but this shot lost nothing by that and Yseult's face was flooded with scarlet at the implied rebuke.

Kathie left it at that and returned to her work, but thereafter Yseult kept her head bent over her books and there was peace for a while. But only for a while. It was left to Heather Clayton who could be thoroughly naughty and tiresome on occasion to cap everything. She was quick enough when she chose and, thanks to what had occurred earlier in the evening, she had worked hard and steadily most of the time. This was unlike her and the reaction came full force as she penned the last word of her essay, capped her pen and dried the final page. She took out her anthology and opened it, for there was still ten minutes of prep to go and she was not minded for a reproof in Miss Ferrar's present condition. Then she felt in her pocket for her handkerchief. It was not there, but something else was.

On the previous Saturday, Intermediate V had a trip to Interlaken in the afternoon. In a shop window they had seen an assortment of those toy creatures which have an end of string hanging from them. If you pull the string and set the article on the floor, it runs. Intermediate V were still childish enough—some of them—to be greatly intrigued and a bunch of them had got permission to invest in some of them.

66

On the Monday evening when work was over, they had amused themselves by trying to get up a race with their latest treasures. It was not a success, seeing that the things all moved on a curve, but it had been good fun. When the bell rang for bed, Heather had thrust hers, an enormous spider whose legs folded in on his body when he was at rest, into the pocket of her frock. She had not worn the frock since, for she had contrived to tear it when she was taking it off and had not been able to mend it until the Thursday evening. She had forgotten all about the spider until now. She took him out and looked at him thoughtfully.

It might have been supposed that the previous events of the evening would have kept her from adding to the list, but with Heather, to think was to do—and at once. It struck her what a joke it would be to let the spider loose at this moment. It *would* create a sensation!

No sooner said than done. Heather set the thing on the ground and yanked the string sharply—more sharply than was at all good for it. At least she must have upset the mechanism, for the eight legs came out and the spider, instead of making a circuit, ran in a dead straight line for the mistress's table.

It was too late to do anything and, in any case, Heather was so stunned by what was happening that she could only sit in her seat in frozen horror. The scratching of the tin legs on the boards attracted the mistress and she looked down. The next moment, she had sprung to her feet with an exclamation. The girls all looked up in amazement, even as she realised what it was and swung forward to snatch it up. Emerence and Con Maynard who both had a horror of spiders, gave a couple of yells and mounted their chairs in a hurry. Some of the others squealed and the rest tittered loudly.

Kathie felt she could have killed herself being so easily caught. Like Emerence and Con, she hated spiders and the thing had been so unexpected that at first sight she had not recognised it as a toy. However, she must stop this noise instantly.

"Girls! Be quiet at once!" she exclaimed as she caught the spider which had not finished the entire length of his run and kicked most realistically in her hand. "It is only a toy which someone has been childish enough to play with. Emerence and Con, come down from those chairs immediately and sit down properly! Not another sound, please, unless you *all* want to be sent to bed early tomorrow night! "

She sounded so angry that the girls fell silent at once. Emerence and Con scrambled down from their perches and sat down, looking remarkably foolish, and Heather realising what she had done, did her best to make amends by owning up at once.

"Pup-please, Miss Ferrars, it was me," she said in English and a very small voice. "I mean—he's mine! "

It was on to this scene that, her lecture finished, the Head arrived in Intermediate V to deal with the offenders in the earliest disturbance of all!

Chapter IX

JOEY MAYNARD MEETS KATHIE

RETRIBUTION fell heavily on all the sinners. By the time Miss Annersley had finished giving them her unbiased opinion of them, Intermediate V were dazedly trying to pick up what was left of themselves. She made no attempt to mince matters nor to spare them a jot of what they deserved. The bell rang for the end of preparation, but she paid no heed to it. It rang ten minutes later for Abendessen and she still went on with her task of reducing the form to a fuller sense of its iniquity. She told them she had had no idea they could be so babyish—and the entire form writhed at the scorn in her voice. She informed them that they had proved themselves untrustworthy and inconsiderate—whereupon more than one girl bit her lips and went darkly red. Then she wanted to know why Francie was standing out.

Francie had to reply for herself, for the question was addressed to her and Miss Annersley heard her with a face that grew grimmer and grimmer.

"Well, Frances," she said when at last Francie had stammered herself to a standstill, "all I can say is that it is clear that you are not yet fit for any Senior form—even the lowest. You may go up to Upper IV for the whole of next week. After that I have to decide whether you remain there or whether we can allow you to come back here. It will depend on yourself."

As Francie had already had to own up to a piece of outrageous impudence to Mary-Lou who, as the Head had not failed to point out, had come to them as her representative, so that the cheeky words and action were, indirectly to Miss Annersley herself, no one was really surprised. All the same, it was the last straw for Francie and she fumbled hurriedly for her handkerchief and did her best to muffle her sobs.

Heather found herself deprived of all Senior privileges for a similar period and came within an ace of following Francie's example. She swallowed hard and clenched her hands and contrived to control herself. But it was a near thing.

The people who, with Francie, had caused the first trouble were told that they might spend the next afternoon in a formal walk instead of joining in the various hockey and netball tests planned for the day. Margot Maynard, who was Shooter for the second netball team and Iris Woodley, who was to have been tried as Goal Defence for the same august body, looked very blue over this. It would mean trouble with Blossom Willoughby, the Games prefect, and Blossom had an unpleasant tongue.

Finally, the Head told the form at large that if this sort of thing continued, she must consider whether she could allow them to count as Seniors or whether she must change the name and status of the form for the rest of the term. Then she swept out, leaving a thoroughly demoralised set of girls behind her for Kathie to dismiss before she fled to wash her hands and go in to Abendessen halfway through the meal.

"Where *have* you been?" Peggy Burnett asked as the new mistress slipped into her seat with a murmured apology and heightened colour. "We wondered if *you* had started a bilious attack, too. In fact," she added blandly, "we were beginning to think that we might be in for an epidemic of gastric flu. Wouldn't we all have blessed you and Joan Bertram if it had been that!"

"Stop teasing!" Miss Derwent interrupted. "You know perfectly well that we saw that Inter V were missing to the last girl. No need to tell us what's been wrong! And, as the Head is also absent, I imagine it's been a bad outbreak." "Simply ghastly!" Kathie replied, applying herself to the bowl of hot soup one of the maids had just set up before her.

The arrival of the Head put a stop to it, for she started them all talking about something else. Meanwhile Kathie worried secretly whether Miss Annersley thought that she was unable to keep order and so unfit for her post. However, that trouble did not last long. By the time everyone was busy with stewed plums and custard, the table was chatting in groups and pairs and Miss Annersley leaned across to Kathie with her most delightful smile and said, "You poor girl! What a time you seem to have been having with those young imps! However, I fancy we've scotched the mischief before it could get any hold. I suppose it was too much to expect that featherheads like Heather and Francie should try to grow up all at once. We'll hope this will be a lesson to them. Those two try to play up every single term and have to be severely crushed. As a rule, though, they behave moderately well thereafter, so I don't think you need worry too much about them. Oh, and by the way, I think you had better confiscate all those absurd toys of theirs and hand them over to Miss Dene. She smiled again and then turned to Mlle sitting next her and slipped easily into a conversation with her, leaving Kathie considerably happier.

When Abendessen was over, she drew the girl into the big entrance hall and chatted gaily with her about two or three things. Then, with kindly eyes on the face that was still rather downcast, she said, "Do stop looking so upset! No one blames you for this silly outbreak. Middles will be Middles and that crowd aren't accustomed yet to considering themselves as Seniors. I fancy they'll think rather more seriously about it after tonight, though."

"They ought to," Kathie agreed, her face brightening. "You certainly dealt faithfully with them!"

Miss Annersley laughed and her blue-grey eyes which had never yet needed glasses, danced with amusement. "Yes; they're all very sorry for themselves. Oh, by the way, if you don't mind, I'd like you to remit your own punishment to the few girls who seem to have had nothing to do with all the uproar. The rest must make up their time, of course; but here's a list of those I should like you to excuse if you will." Then she added with another of those flashing smiles, "I'm very sorry you have to punish yourself as well. But that often happens to us though no girl ever seems to realise it. However, you won't have much difficulty after this for some time to come."

Kathie took the list and glanced at it. Len—Jo—Con—Rosamund—Joan—Alicia—and Janet Kemp, one of the new girls. She looked up at the Head. "Of course I'll excuse them. I'm afraid I was so angry I didn't trouble to make any distinction. I just lumped them all together."

"One tends to do that in such circumstances," the Head agreed. "All the same, it's always well to avoid any appearance of injustice. Girls of their age are always ready to scent it—and resent it—I'm *not* making a pun!" she added hastily, laughing.

Kathie joined in the laugh. "I couldn't imagine you doing such a thing, Miss Annersley. Thank you for warning me. I'll remember after this."

"Good! Well, this evening's contretemps won't have done anyone any harm. Francie Wilford certainly deserves all she's getting and so does Heather—though Jo informed me so earnestly that Heather owned up at once before you even asked."

Kathie suddenly giggled as she remembered Heather's stricken expression. "She did—oh, she *did*! And I'm convinced that she never meant the thing to head for me as it did. She looked positively pussystruck at the time."

"I can believe it!" the Head said drily. "Heather is completely thoughtless, but she is a really nice girl at bottom. You'll find Francie a very different proposition, I'm afraid. She's a good deal of a problem to all of us. Try to keep you patience with her. But always be firm. We've tried leniency with her and it didn't answer at all. She simply became more outrageous. Make her respect you, though. She's a girl who can be ruled that way more easily than any other.

"And now I've something much pleasanter to tell you. I know you've heard plenty about Joey Maynard from next door—mother to the triplets. She rang up early today to tell me she wants you to go over and have 'English tea' with her on Sunday."

Kathie looked shy. "But—did she mean *alone*? I've never met her."

The Head gave her a twinkly look. "Oh, my dear girl, you can't possibly feel shy with Joey. It just can't be done! She wouldn't allow it. Run along to the office and give her a ring and tell her you're coming—or shall I do it for you?" she added as her keen gaze saw the pink deepening in Kathie's cheeks.

"Oh—would you *mind*?" Kathie murmured confusedly.

"Of course not. I'll leave Joey herself to prove to you that I'm right, though. There isn't time now. Run along and have your coffee, child, or you'll miss it altogether, thanks to Francie's ill-doings. I'll see to Joey."

Kathie thanked the Head and went off and Miss Annersley turned off to the study where she rang up the school's most beloved Old Girl to inform her that she might expect her visitor on Sunday.

"Good!" came the reply. "What Hilda? Shy of me—of *me*! Good Heavens! Who on earth am *I* for anyone to be shy of?"

"Your English," Miss Annersley said dispassionately, "is horrible. No one would think you'd ever been taught anything."

A peal of golden laughter reached her over the telephone. She heard the telephone receiver clatter as Joey hung up with a click and went to collect her books for Prayers, smiling to herself.

Somehow Intermediate V got through the rest of the evening. With Miss Ferrars sitting before them, correcting exercises in grim silence, they applied themselves to their work with such a will that most of them contrived to get through quite a good deal. Finally, she let all of them go, but Francie who sat sullenly at her desk. She dared not waste her time. The punishment already awarded her prevented that. When at last, half-an-hour before her bed-time, Miss Ferrars told her to put her books away and go along to the common room. she was in a state of suppressed rebellion. She put the books into her desk and left the room still in sulky silence. Once she was with her fellows, however, the pent-up fury broke.

"It's the limit!" she cried to Betty Landon, quite forgetting the business about Len. "Honestly, I think *all* mistresses are positively inhuman!"

Betty's reply was not soothing. With a very chilly look she said, "The less *you* say about inhuman behaviour, the more you'll shine! What about the way you left Len to bear the blame for your kiddish pellet-throwing? And never owned up! Or not till Miss Ferrars asked point blank I should have thought you'd know by now just how we look at such things. Anyhow, no one wants much to do with you."

Francie held her tongue because she had nothing to say. But she thought the more. By the time they were all summoned to bed, she was literally seething. And the worst of it was that she dared not let her wrath loose in case the Head heard of it and left her down in Upper IV for another year.

During Saturday, the rest of them behaved like budding angels. Francie was not openly defiant, but she sulked industriously the whole day. The afternoon walk was a very prim affair, for Mlle de Lachenais took charge and she let the entire party feel itself in disgrace by wrapping herself up in a mantle of icy dignity that was very unlike jolly little Mlle. Further, when she spoke to them, she spoke in French and insisted that they should reply in the same language. This on a Saturday when they were usually allowed to speak in any language they chose, was adding insult to injury and the walk was, on the whole, a silent one.

On the Sunday afternoon Kathie, wishing heartily that she had never said she would go, set off for Freudesheim, the Maynard's house. It was a chilly October day, for the clouds had come down during the night and though the mist on the Görnetz Platz was thin enough not to be dangerous, it was damp and chilling. Kathie wrapped herself up in her big winter coat and an enormous scarf and set off down the drive, her heart in her boots. Biddy o'Ryan had advised her to cut through the two gardens which were linked by a gate in the dividing hedge of arbor vitæ, but she refused to do that. So she left the big gates, walked briskly along the curving road and turned down to the white gate leading into the Maynard's house. Nearly rigid with shyness, she crawled up the drive and arrived at the foot of the steps leading up to the house. The front door flew open and a tall dark woman, with a delicate, mobile face under a deep straight fringe of black hair stood at the top of the steps, holding out welcoming hands.

"Come up—come up!" cried a golden voice. "Hurry up and come in out of the cold and damp! Don't, for goodness sake, stand there being polite in this weather! What a change from yesterday!" She pulled her guest into the hall and slammed the door behind them. "Come and hang your things up. Why didn't you cut across the

73

gardens? My eyes nearly fell out when I saw you at the gate! *No* one at the school ever treats me with such prim manners. Besides, it's yards nearer."

"I—I didn't like to," Kathie stammered as she got rid of her wraps.

"Well, don't ever do it again! Ready? Then come along to the salon. We've had an open grate put in this last summer and we've got a gorgeous fire waiting to welcome you. I hope you like babies, by the way? And dogs, too? Because I always have my babies to myself till bedtime on Sundays and my St. Bernard, Bruno, goes pretty well everywhere with me. Come and meet the lot!" Joey chattered as she ushered the visitor into a great room that ran from back to front of the house with a fireplace opposite the side window where a glorious wood fire was blazing away behind the high guard and two tiny, very fair people were building houses in a corner while in a basket framed playpen, a six months old baby lay gurgling and kicking.

"You know my triplets. They're in your form, I hear. And here are my twins," Joey said as the primrose-fair pair jumped up and scampered across the floor to her. "This is Felicity and the boy is Felix. Say 'How do you do', darlings."

Felicity greeted the stranger very prettily, but Felix, at four, was growing manly and he shied away from Kathie's offered kiss. "I don't kiss girls," he said.

"Then shake hands," his mother said. "No one wants to kiss you if you don't want it, Felix, but you must mind your manners, my lad."

Felix shook hands and then rushed back to his building. His twin followed him and Joey, with a grin, informed her visitor, "That's just how his cousin David Russell treated me years ago when I was still at school and he was Felix's age." She stooped over the playpen and scooped up the baby. "Never mind him! Admire our latest instead. There! What do you think of *that* for an effort!"

She exhibited the baby proudly and Kathie admired the silky dark curls, the dark eyes with their absurdly long lashes and the pink cheeks each with a dimple in it. "Rather nice, isn't she? Would you like to take her?

She sat Kathie down in a low chair by the fire and put the baby in her arms. "There! What do you think of her?"

74

"Oh, she's lovely!" Kathie cried, all her shyness gone in face of this friendly warmth. "She's so soft and cuddly! But isn't she unlike the twins!" she added with a glance to the corner where the two flaxen heads were bobbing about.

"Oh, quite. You see, I'm very dark and I had the luck to marry a fair man so we have no monotony in our family. Con and this small thing and Charles, our second boy, are all dark. Steve, Mike and those two are fair, though the twins are the fairest of the lot. And Margot and Len are red, though even then it isn't the same. Len's chestnut and Margot's golden red. And they're just as unlike in character—as I expect you know where the three girls are concerned. Did you ever know triplets more unlike each other?"

"I've never known triplets before," Kathie said demurely.

Joey laughed. "I don't suppose you have. I'll show you the boys' latest photo. You'll probably meet Mike. He comes up for week-ends at present, though when the real winter weather begins, that'll have to stop. Here you are. The big one is Steve; that's Charles; this curly-top is Mike. Not much alike each other, are they?"

"No," Kathie agreed as she studied the photograph. "Mike's like Margot, though."

"How right you are! And it's more than looks!" quoth their mother darkly. "Mike has as big a share of mischief as Margot. And Felix is turning like him—Twins! I hear Bruno whining at the front door. Run and let him in, will you?"

The twins dropped their bricks and scampered off and she turned to Kathie and said with a chuckle, "Yesterday, Felix had been very naughty and disobedient. I was talking very seriously to him when it suddenly dawned on me that he wasn't paying much attention. I said, 'Felix!' No reply. 'Felix!' Still no reply. 'Felix! I'm speaking to you!' And he replied, very distantly, 'I fink we won't discuss vis any longer'."

Kathie burst into a peal of laughter while Joey took the baby from her and grinned at her. "Neat, wasn't it. Of course he didn't get away with it. I kept a straight face and rebuked him pretty sharply. But I can tell you it was an effort."

"It must have been," Kathie said, still chuckling.

Then the door burst open and a handsome gentleman in a very damp coat of gold and white tore into the room and tried to fling himself on his mistress who retreated promptly behind a chair. Foiled, he turned his attention to Kathie and had washed her face very thoroughly before Joey had managed to call him off.

"Bruno—Bruno! Sit down! Lie down!" She crossed to put the baby back in the playpen and turned to Kathie. "I'm most awfully sorry. He's young and silly and abnormally affectionate." She paused to rub behind the beautifully set ears as Bruno thrust his head against her and beat the guest over the knees with his flail-like tail. Joey laughed. "All the same, I'll bet you aren't feeling shy with me now. It's impossible for anyone to do so in *this* house. What with dogs who go mad and small folk who come out with the most unexpected remarks, my only wonder is that anyone cares to come and visit us. Let's go and see about tea, twins. Kathie—I'm going to call you that straight away—can you keep an eye on Cecil for me? And you might pull up that little table for the twins and those two small chairs if you will."

She departed, escorted by the twins and Bruno, and Kathie did as she was asked and then knelt down by the playpen to hold a conversation with Cecil who gurgled and cooed cheerfully at her, looking the picture of a contented baby.

Felicity, stumping back with a dish of cakes, came to join her. "Isn't she pwetty Auntie Kaffie?"

"She's lovely," Kathie said.

The trolley was wheeled into the room by a proud Felix. Joey followed, laying a hand to guide it round traps of rugs with which the floor was scattered. Then they sat down to tea, Joey remarking, "I'm a spoiled woman when all my boys are at home. My husband has always insisted that as soon as they're old enough they learn to wait on me. I'm sorry you won't meet him today, but he was called out to a village up in the mountains and told me to expect him when I saw him. So it may be midnight before he returns."

It was a delicious tea with cakes from one of the pâtesseries in Montreux—wafer bread and butter and tea that was rich with cream. When it was over the Coadjutor, a young Swiss girl who helped Anna, the Maynards' factotum, arrived to bear off the twins to the playroom for

76

the short time left before their early bedtime. When they had gone, the two ladies pulled up their chairs to the fire and Joey initiated a delightful talk about the school.

In the course of it, she gathered something of the situation between the young mistress and Mary-Lou Trelawney. She looked first startled and then grave, but she made no comment. She told of her own schooldays and kept Kathie in fits of laughter over the adventures she related. Finally, she whisked her off to help with bedtime and by the time the twins were safely in bed and Joey herself had carried Cecil to her own room to attend to her needs, the girl felt a stranger no longer.

"I've had a gorgeous time," she said when the grandfather clock in the hall chimed seven and she had to go. "Thank you so much, Mrs. Maynard."

"My name's Joey," that lady said promptly. "Might as well begin as you're bound to end. Are you sure you can find your way back?"

"Oh, yes. The mist's thinning out and there's a young moon, too."

"O.K. Go through the gardens."

"Very well. Thanks so much for my lovely visit."

"Go across the lawn and through the gate in the hedge. That brings you out on a path. Goodbye, Kathie. Come again soon. I want you to meet my husband."

She stood on the step, the light from the hall outlining her tall, graceful figure, waving until Kathie was out of sight. Then she went in and rang up the school. "That you, Hilda? I like your Kathie Ferrars. She's got a lot to learn, poor lamb, but you keep hold of her. It's all there when she's got a little more sense and she's going to make the kind of mistress we like to have in the school."

Chapter X

MARY-LOU

INTERMEDIATE V having been effectually suppressed, it was to be expected that the rest of the school would, as Miss Derwent announced one evening in the Staffroom "read, mark, learn, and inwardly digest" what had happened and profit by it.

"And *that's* asking for trouble if you do like! " Peggy Burnett murmured to Miss Moore. "After tempting Providence like that, look out for squalls! "

Rosalind Moore laughed. "Hardly, with my own crowd. They're being very grown-up and superior these days."

"Are you telling me?" Nancy Wilmot chipped in. "You know it's odd, but if there is anything more elderly than a mid-teenager, I'd like to hear of it."

"The natural reaction from having been wild and wicked Middles," Miss Derwent laughed. "They go to the other extreme. The swing of the pendulum, my dear."

"It doesn't seem to have had much effect on my own demons," Kathie said ruefully. "Oh, they're behaving like a set of unfledged archangels at the moment, but how long it'll last, goodness only knows! "

"For the rest of the term," Biddy o'Ryan assured her. "Sure, I know what it's like when the Head takes to skinning you with her tongue. Bill was bad enough—but even Bill could never better the Abbess for gentle irony, once she gets really going! To judge by the snatches of chat I've been hearing, the Head nearly took the skin off your little darlings, Kathie."

"She did that all right," Kathie asserted.

"Serve them right, too! I'm sorry for people like Jo Scott and Len and Con Maynard and Rosamund Lilley who are all more or less law-abiding as a rule. However, it won't hurt them, even if they didn't deserve it."

"I *was* there," Kathie replied. "I thought my old Head at the High could say plenty when she was aroused, but I must say Miss Annersley has her beaten to a frazzle! You know," she went on to one in particular, "with her lovely voice I could never have believed it of her. 'Icy' simply doesn't describe her tones. They made *me* shiver. I don't wonder the girls were crushed to flinders when she had gone."

Nancy chuckled. "My dear, you didn't have the privilege of being a pupil at this school and I did. I can believe anything in that line from her when she's really mad. How she used to make me writhe when I was a kid!"

Mlle looked up from her embroidery. "And that, did you no harm. And she knew just how much sarcasm to use and who would mind bitterly and who would be, as you say, too thick-skinned to worry about it. Me, I think that sarcasm is a very good weapon when used with discretion; but it is necessary to be careful in using it."

"Hear that, you youngsters?" Peggy asked of Kathie, Sharlie, and Joan Bertram who had recovered from her bilious attack and was back in school again. "Beware how you use sarcasm and to whom."

Miss Derwent backed her up in this. "It can be all to the good when used sparingly; but don't use it too often or it loses its edge—and not at all if it's to a sensitive child." She swung round on Peggy Burnett. "And who may you be to be calling people 'youngsters', I'd like to know? It isn't so very long since you were Staff baby yourself. A little less condescension, if you please!"

Peggy shrieked and hid her face. "Spare me—oh, spare me! Consider it unsaid, you three! I wouldn't hurt your feelings for any money."

The Staff burst out laughing and then Rosalie Dene arrived after a long session on the telephone with a parent, and the conversation went off to other topics.

Being exceedingly busy, what with her ordinary form work and all the extra coaching she was giving Yseult, Kathie forgot the talk before she went to bed, which was a pity. She did not like Yseult though she consciously tried to let that make no difference to her treatment of the girl, and had decided that the sooner she was moved up from Inter V the better for all concerned. Yseult was a bad mixer. She went round with a perpetual chip on her shoulder and grumbled at all the work she was expected to do. Matron's fiat about her hair held, but Yseult complained bitterly every time she had to tie it back which did not endear her to her dormitory. The two younger girls had settled down amazingly well, but their sister was against everybody and everything connected with the Chalet School. Sarcasm was no use with her. She simply did not see it and Kathie never used it to her. But she did give every moment she could spare during working hours to the thankless task of "getting Yseult on".

"I only hope that lazy monkey Yseult is grateful to you for all the work you're putting on her," Biddy o'Ryan remarked one day when they were nearing half-term. "The way you've slogged at her, she ought to be thankful."

Kathie laughed. "I don't think gratitude for that sort of thing is *in* Yseult. She's a tiresome, sulky creature and, if you want to know, I'm only doing it to shove her off on to someone else. She and Francie Wilford are the plagues of my life. Francie is either sullen when I long to shake her; or she comes as near downright impudence as she dares—and then I yearn to box her ears. As for Yseult, her airs and graces make me utterly tired!"

"What a diatribe." Biddy said lightly. "My good child you'll be coming up against this sort of thing as long as you teach. The only thing to do is to have your ordinary patience and cultivate about twice as much to deal with them."

"It's all very well talking," Kathie said crossly, "but *you* don't have those two perpetually on your chest. I can do with imps like Heather and Margot and even Emerence Hope. They do have spasms of trying to pull up and if they're demons on occasion they're *nice* demons. But Yseult and Francie are utter pests."

"Oh, I've me own trials," Biddy confessed solemnly. "They're not like yours, I'll admit; but they're trials all the same. Verity Carey is a born mooner, worse than Con Maynard except when Con gets buried in a story or an epic or whatever it is she's writing. Then, as Joey says, she's good for neither man nor beast. But with Verity it goes on nearly all the time. Heaven help any man who thinks of marrying her! And Nina Rutherford does try most of the time, but it's easy to see where her mind is. That's the worst of being a genius!"

"A genius? I should just think so! My goodness, how that girl can play!" Kathie exclaimed, forgetting her crossness. "I had to go into Hall last night to put up a notice for the Head. She was practising and I don't mind owning that I simply dropped on to the nearest chair and sat there listening to her for twenty solid minutes. I never heard anything like her—for her age! "

The talk ceased and Kathie went off to take Upper IV through the great ocean currents while Biddy, who was free that period, settled down to some badly overdue corrections.

This was on the Wednesday. Next day, which was "German" day, and which Kathie disliked, since her German was by no means as fluent as her French, Miss Moore came up to her at the middle of Break.

"You're free last period this morning, aren't you?" she asked. "Well," as Kathie nodded, "would you do me a great favour and take Lower VI for me then? I've just seen Matey and she's told me that she's managed to make an appointment for me with Herr Leichen, but it's for fourteen o'clock. That means I'll have to have something to eat early and catch the twelve-thirty train to Interlaken. I wouldn't worry, but this wretched tooth is giving me no peace. I'll simply have to have it seen to and he can't take me any other time till the end of next week. You don't mind, do you?"

She might well ask, for Kathie was looking apalled.

"But—Lower VI! " she protested. "Couldn't you just set them work and leave them to get on with it."

"I'd do that, only they've had to miss two or three lessons lately for one reason or another and if you *will* do it, I'd be everlasting grateful to you."

Kathie looked undecided. Miss Moore urged the case more strongly. "Why can't you do it? I'm sure you're capable of teaching them and they're a very nice set. Hilda Jukes is a giggler, though goodness knows she tries to control it, poor soul! Felicity King has just realised that she's by way of being a pretty girl and Meg Whyte has no brains. Still, take them all in all, they're a nice crowd. You'll have no trouble."

Kathie sighed inwardly; but Miss Moore was really looking pulled down with the pain of the nagging tooth and she couldn't refuse, especially as she was free at the time. "Very well. I'll do my best and saints can't do more. What work are they to do?"

"It's commercial geography today," Miss Moore said with a hand pressed to her aching cheek. "I was going to go on with revision on the effects of configuration on natural products. They did it pretty thoroughly in the Fifth last year. It really is only revision. Start them off with an odd question and keep them going when they seem to be side-tracking. For the most part, they'll go over it by discussion. I always encourage that at their stage. I think they remember much better if they thrash it out among themselves. They're using Australia for illustration."

"I think I can manage that all right," Kathie said. "All right; I'll take it over. I only hope Herr Leichen can give you some relief. Rosalind! You're *black* under the eyes! Did you get *any* sleep last night?"

"Not much," Miss Moore admitted. "None after four o'clock. Thanks a lot, Kathie. I'll do the same for you any time, so don't be shy of asking."

Then the bell rang for the end of Break and they had to go to their work.

It was with some quakings that Kathie collected her books and went to Lower VI at the end of the morning. These elder girls were so near herself in age that she felt nervous about teaching them. She reminded herself that they *were* only schoolgirls and she was a university graduate, but it didn't seem to help much. Then she gathered her gown about her and stalked into the room, looking considerably more sure of herself than she felt.

As she deposited her books on the table, she glanced round and it struck her what a pretty room it was. It was full of the late October sunshine and the broad windowsills were laden with vases of flowers and flowering plants. The pictures on the walls were tinted reproductions of paintings by Birket Foster, Constable, Cox and other artists of the English countryside.

There were eleven girls in VIb that year, ranging from Bess Appleton who was nearly eighteen and looking forward to going on to St. Mildred's at the end of the year, to Mary-Lou Trelawney who had been sixteen at the end of the previous June. After people like the Maynards, not yet thirteen, and girls of fourteen and fifteen like Jo Scott, Rosamund Lilley, Heather Clayton and Co.. they seemed quite elderly. She noted Felicity King and agreed that she *was* pretty. But with lovely Vi Lucy, Lesley Malcolm with her well-cut features and air of distinction, Hilary Bennet's charming face, full of character and—she had to own it if she were honest—Mary-Lou's promise of extreme good looks, she saw nothing in Felicity to make that young lady become absorbed in herself.

They rose as one girl when the mistress entered and remained standing until she told them to sit down. She noticed that they had everything ready they were likely to need and they all sat upright and ready, though their faces questioned her appearance.

"I'm sorry to have to tell you," she began, "that Miss Moore has to go to visit the dentist this afternoon, so I'm taking her place for once. She tells me that she wants us to revise the effect of the relief of land on natural products with special attention to Australia. Will you take your synthetic maps of relief and products, please. And if you want to make any notes, have pencils and notebooks handy as well."

The girls produced them and then sat looking at their new mistress expectantly. How would she compare with Miss Moore whose lessons were so interesting?

Kathie knew this and it increased her nervousness. However, she knew her subject well. "Look first at your relief maps and note the run of the mountain ranges and the rivers," she said. "Take particular note of where the rivers lie, and the lakes. If you like to use your climate maps as well, have them at hand."

This would have been a signal in Intermediate V for rustling of maps, scuffling and general disturbance. Vlb simply produced the maps with a minimum of trouble and sat looking at them.

"Now," said Kathie, "superimpose natural products on relief and correlate them."

Hilda Jukes, an amiable, but by no means clever girl, looked puzzled at the unusual word. Mary-Lou sitting next her caught the bewilderment in her face.

"She only means see how they are related," she muttered as she squared her own maps accurately.

Kathie overheard and was down on the girl like a shot. "That will do, Mary-Lou. If you have anything to say, please say it to me."

Mary-Lou flushed, but she bent over her maps in silence. Hilda spoke up. "I didn't understand just what you meant, Miss Ferrars," she said, "and Mary-Lou was only explaining to me."

"Then you should have asked me," Kathie said

inflexibly. She was determined to give the girls no chance of playing her up.

They were all much too senior to exchange glances, but Hilary Bennet's eyebrows shot up into her curly hair and Felicity King opened her eyes widely. Kathie felt herself going pink. She must not forget that these were very senior girls and probably accustomed to much more freedom than could be permitted to her own crowd.

"It's very difficult! " she thought. "I *must* keep my dignity and yet I don't want to pull the reins too tight." And she began the lesson with a question to Lesley Malcolm as to the areas of Australia which were given to agriculture.

Lesley knew and answered promptly and clearly. Presently the lesson was in full swing and Kathie left the girls to a free discussion.

As in most good modern schools, they had been taught to reason and think things out for themselves. The talk flew round the room and gradually the rather tense atmosphere in which the lesson had begun was tempered and they were arguing among themselves and appealing to her at intervals. Presently, someone mooted the question of the Australian deserts and asked the young mistress if nothing could be done to make them productive.

"That is one of Australia's biggest problems," Kathie replied, "If it could be solved, the land could carry twice as big a population and produce at least twice as much. But so far, they haven't been able to do much about it."

"There *are* water courses marked here and there," Mary-Lou said thoughtfully. "Wouldn't it be possible to dam some of the rivers and turn them into reservoirs and then pipe the water through to irrigate the desert land?"

"That's what they're going to do with the new Snowy River dam they're building, isn't it, Miss Ferrars?" Bess inquired. "If they can do it there, why not in the northern territories?"

"It's partly a question of climate. They have a fairly heavy rainfall in Victoria and it is mountainous as well. Then you must remember the difference in geographical position. The Northern Territories lie in the equatorial zone which means tremendous heat. There isn't enough natural water to give rise to condensation, so very little rain."

"But Miss Ferrars, they have awful floods in Queensland, don't they?" Mary-Lou had bobbed up again. "Wouldn't it be possible to erect dams across the head waters of the rivers and convert them into reservoirs and then pipe the water west?"

"That would kill two birds with one stone," Lesley added. "It would help the Northern Territories and wouldn't it prevent the terrible floods in the east?"

"You forget the enormous distances," Kathie said, trying hard to forget that to her mind Mary-Lou, at any rate, was a bumptious young thing who needed a good setting-down. "I suppose it *could* be done—if they could find the money."

"How could they do that?" Bess wanted to know.

"Well, I'm sure they couldn't do it out of annual revenue. I suppose they might try to float a loan. But it would be a very chancy thing and they might find they couldn't get enough support to make it worth while."

"Then isn't there *any* way of getting over it?" Lesley Bethune demanded.

"I think only if they could pump it up from the great underground lake that is known to lie there."

"How do they know about it?" Meg Whyte asked.
She was a great friend of Hilda Jukes' and generally disputed with that young woman for the bottom of the form.

"By sinking wells in different areas. Also by studying the geological formations," Kathie explained. "But don't think it either easy or cheap to sink these wells. It means going down to great depths and even so, the water isn't always available."

" 'Great depths'?" Lesley Malcolm said thoughtfully. "How deep are some of the wells, Miss Ferrars?"

"There is one at a place called Whitewood which goes down to 5,045 feet. Some go down for over a thousand feet—there is one that goes to 1,645 feet, I remember. They do produce a tremendous volume of water, but you have to remember that most of them are on the borders of the desert and so not much good to the central part. The water's there, all right, but it's too difficult and much too costly to bring it to the surface for anyone to attempt it—at present, at any rate." Then she added, "if you want to know any more about it, consult the Encyclopedia.

Meanwhile, let's go on to grasses which are quite as important."

"Just one more question," Mary-Lou pleaded. "What makes the water rise in the borings, Miss Ferrars? Is it the result of suction?"

"In most places, it rises because of the gases in the earth. The borings release them as well as the water and their power forces the water up along with them. You may like to know, girls," Kathie added, "that there is at least one town in Australia which not only gets its water from a boring, but all the gas for lighting and heating. And now that's enough. Hilary, what is the tallest grass known in Australia?"

Hilary had been dreaming and she jumped when she heard her name. Not being prepared with an answer, she simply looked blank. Mary-Lou, as always, leapt into the breach at once. "Isn't it the sugar cane?" She asked.

Kathie eyed her severely. "I spoke to Hilary. Is *your* name Hilary by any chance?"

Mary-Lou flushed. The mistress's tone was cutting and she loathed sarcasm. "I beg your pardon," she said.

"I should think so. Please let other people have a chance to answer a *few* questions. I expect they know quite as much as you if you will only leave them to speak for themselves," Kathie replied, that sarcastic inflection still edging her tones. "There are eleven people in this form, Mary-Lou—not one."

Mary-Lou was darkly red by this time, but she said no more and Kathie repeated the question to Hilary who mumbled something and then sat back. The lesson continued, but it had lost its spontaneity. The girls waited to be asked questions and free discussion was at an end. Mary-Lou was a great favourite with her own clan and they all, without exception, resented the tone the new mistress had taken to her. Admitted, she was a prize butter-in, as Lesley Bethune remarked later on; but though any other mistress would have curbed her eagerness, none of them would have used just that tone to her.

It did Mary-Lou no real harm to know that she wasn't going to get away with things as she so frequently did. She was hurt at the moment for she was unable to imagine what she could have done to annoy Miss Ferrars. But she was a level-headed girl and her own view, as expressed to a select audience of Vi Lucy, Hilary and the two Lesleys when they were free to chatter was that if the mistress didn't like her, well that was just too bad, but she didn't see what she could do about it at present.

"Mary-Lou! What are you planning?" Vi exclaimed with apprehension well founded.

"I've told you I don't know—yet. It'll have to wait," was the unsatisfactory reply.

"If you've any sense, you'll leave it alone," Lesley Bethune said bluntly.

"Not me! Some time I'm going to find out what I've done to give her such a hate at me," Mary-Lou returned with fine simplicity. "But it'll have to wait till after half-term, at any rate. With our Evening coming next Saturday, I've got all on my plate that I can manage at present, anyhow. And what are we going to *do* for half-term? Does anyone know *that* yet?"

No one did, but it successfully side-tracked Vi and the others from the question of Miss Ferrars as she had intended.

However, that came later. At the time, the end of the lesson dragged and Kathie was thankful when the bell rang for the end of morning school. She told the girls to make notes on the lesson to show up to Miss Moore at her next session with them, gathered up her books and departed. Unfortunately, instead of blaming herself as she should have done, she blamed Mary-Lou. The girl was bumptious and forward and selfish into the bargain. She was so anxious to show off the extent of her own knowledge that she never gave anyone else a chance. Also, she was far too familiar in her manners. Why on earth everyone else seemed to like her so much was a mystery to Kathie.

"I don't see anything much to like in her," she thought as she hung up her gown and went to wash her hands. "If I had much to do with her I'd sooner bring her down a few pegs!"

So it was just as well that she neither had much to do with Mary-Lou nor was likely to—in school, at any rate.

Chapter XI

THE PREFECTS ENTERTAIN

KATHIE was accustomed now to the Saturday evening entertainments when the Houses took it in turn to play hostesses to the rest of the school. But on the Monday following the trouble in VIb, an invitation came from the prefects to the Staff for Saturday Evening that week.

"How do they entertain us?" Kathie was curious about this.

"But chérie, that depends on how much originality they have among them," Mlle de Lachennais responded as she joined them.

"I'm expecting the worst," Miss Lawrence, put in gloomily. "Have you observed the note at the bottom— 'Please wear your very worst'. Those young monkeys are up to something! "

"I'll go in my old blue," Biddy observed. "It's on its last legs, anyhow, so if their minds are running in the direction of making us cockfight or have rolling races on the floor, 'twon't matter at all, at all."

Kathie, with a completly new outfit, pulled a long face over this. "But *all* my things are new. What shall I do about it?"

"Wire home for something—and ask them to send it by airmail," Sharlie Andrews suggested. "It'll be in plenty of time if they send off at once. This is only Monday. Ask them to send your worst, though."

Kathie took the advice with the result that on the Thursday morning, a parcel arrived for her by airmail. The frock Mrs. Grayson had chosen belonged to her last year at school and she had forgotten all about it. It had been a charming rose-pink,. but she had nose-bled copiously all down the front and ruined it. It had been stuck at the back of her closet and now, nearly five years later, was out of date, faded a little and with those awful streaks was quite unwearable from an everyday point of view.

Saturday, when it came, was gloriously fine and the girls were able to play off inter-House netball and hockey matches so that everyone was well occupied. Kaffee und Kuchen came at half-past sixteen, and when it was over, the Staff and prefects fled to change in readiness for what lay ahead. The invitation was from eighteen o'clock to twenty-two with an interval at nineteen o'clock to allow the people responsible for school Prayers to slip out. At ten minutes to eighteen the mistresses began to assemble in their own sitting-room and many and pithy were the comments on their attire.

"Well, isn't it time we were making a move?" Miss Wilson, who had been especially invited, suggested.

"Quite time," Miss Annersley agreed. "Come along, Nell! We'll lead off. The rest of you follow in twos and threes so that our hostesses aren't overwhelmed at once."

She left the room with her hand slipped through Miss Wilson's arm and the others followed in small groups at intervals of two or three minutes. Kathie found herself making a threesome with Biddy o'Ryan and Nancy Wilmot, while Sharlie trotted after with Miss Denny and Frau Mieders, two of the oldest on the Staff.

Saturday Evenings always took place in Hall. The mistresses ran lightly down the front stairs, thankful that the girls would not see them in their disreputable attire, and giggling at themselves as they went. Biddy tapped at the top door of Hall and it was opened by Blossom Willoughby. She and the rest of her clan had all sent home for the old summer frocks they had worn when the school was on St. Briavel's island and the brown-checked ginghams with white collars and cuffs and flame-coloured ties were all clean enough, but in most cases distinctly on the short and tight side. Mary-Lou had grown enormously during the previous Christmas term as the result of a bad accident and she had had to spend all the afternoon turning up the bottom of hers with a false hem and even now it was barely decent.

"We thought you might like to see our old uniform again," Elinor Pennell explained when the two Heads exclaimed at it.

When the last mistress had arrived, the doors were shut and Elinor, from the platform, requested the guests to stand in a wide circle. When they were all in place, the prefects formed a solemn procession and marched round them, pausing before each one to eye her from head to foot before making a note in the tiny books they all carried.

"You're making me feel nervous!" Miss Wilson, commonly known as "Bill" to her unregenerate pupils, protested. "What's it all in aid of? We've only done what you asked us to do and put on our worst."

"You'll see later," Mary-Lou told her with an irrepressible grin.

"Impudent hussy!" said "Bill" amiably. "Mary-Lou, *what* are you going to do with us?"

But neither Mary-Lou nor Hilary who was with her would speak and she had to wait for their time while they passed on to Matron who wore an aged and faded uniform which had seen its best days when the school was in Tirol. The years had made her thinner, so it was distinctly on the large side, though crisp and spotless as usual.

"Well, you won't look so spick and span at the end of the evening," Mary-Lou told her with a broad grin.

"Knowing you girls, I'm quite aware of that fact!" Matron returned.

At last the review ended and the mistresses were requested to sit down while the giggling prefects clustered together in a body for a brief consultation. Then Elinor mounted the dais again and asked them to take partners and form a procession. That done, the girls themselves paired off and headed the line while Mlle Lenoir with whom Elinor and Leila Norris, the second prefect, had had a long confab that afternoon, went to the piano. She had to be excused anything strenuous in any case as a slip on the stair had resulted in a strained ankle two days ago.

"This," Elinor announced blandly, "is FOLLOW MY LEADER. Leila and I lead and there's a prize for the couple who last longest. If you break the following you're out and go and sit down. Do you mind, Mlle Lenoir?"

Mlle Lenoir began to play a slow march and they stalked round the room at a funereal pace. She stopped and went off into waltz time, when the Leaders solemnly waltzed away from each other and then back before taking hands and swinging round and round at a giddy pace. This was too much for Miss Annersley and she took Matron out of it in short order; but the rest stayed the course, though "Bill" murmured to Nancy Wilmot, "That weak foot of mine isn't going to stand much of this sort of thing!"

The next was a one-two-three-hop which was easy

enough; but it was followed by leapfrog across your partner which removed most of the older mistresses before it had gone very far. As "Bill" said when she sat down and mopped her streaming face. "I'm as agile as most women of my age, but I bar leapfrog!"

Worse was to follow. The Leaders each raised her inside leg and her partner clutched the ankle with her outside hand while each slung her inside arm round her partner's waist. Thus linked, they hopped—or tried to! —across the top of the room and this did finish off most of the Staff, leaving only Nancy Wilmot who was paired with Joan Bertram, and Kathie and Sharlie, Biddy and Davida Armitage.

"I never knew that I had so many contortionists on the Staff before," said Miss Annersley, watching their antics with deep interest.

The next effort was to lie down flat on your tummy and *inch* your way by dint of using your elbows, whereat, Biddy and Davida gave it up, leaving Nancy Wilmot and the three youngsters to turn a series of handsprings, keeping level with partners as they did it. Kathie lost time, so she and Sharlie were disqualified and this left Nancy Wilmot and Joan Bertram as winners.

"Just as well we stopped there," the former remarked as she borrowed pins to pin up a long three-cornered tear in the skirt of her dress. "They'd have had the clothes off our backs with anything more!"

"I think it's just as well you warned us to wear our very worst," Miss Annersley said to Lesley Bethune when that young woman came to sit down beside her. "What an appalling ordeal for a set of respectable mistresses!"

"Never mind," Lesley said soothingly. "The next is a sitting-down event."

"But me, I must wash!" cried Mlle de Lachennais, regarding her grubby hands with dismay.

"Not till supper time," Nan Herbert, the editor of the *Chaletian*, told her firmly. "We're going to have a round of SCANDAL now. Pull your chairs a little close, everyone. We're rather too far apart."

This done, Mary-Lou started the game by whispering a long story into Miss Denny's ear to the accompaniment of protests. "You're tickling me, Mary-Lou!"—"I can't hear half you're saying!" and so on.

"That's the idea," Mary-Lou said demurely, having

91

finished her story. "Now you pass on as much as you heard in a whisper to Sybil."

The story passed on its round, altering considerably as it went. Miss Annersley was the last and her face when she heard what Bess Appleton, punctuating her words with wild giggles, had to whisper, was a study!

"Tell us what you heard!" Mary-Lou cried eagerly.

"Well, I *hope* this isn't what Mary-Lou began with," the Head said as she stood up. "What I *got* was—at least, I *think* it was—'Miss Dene was on the stairs and she was a cannibal'!"

"What?" exclaimed the maligned Miss Dene.

"Well, that's what I *heard,*" the Head said defensively. "Now, Mary-Lou!"

Mary-Lou stood up in such a state of giggles that it was nearly a minute before she could speak. "What I said was, 'One morning, Emerence wanted to come down the front stairs, but Miss Dene caught her and sent her to the back stairs, only she wouldn't go. Then Miss Dene walked her to the back stairs and told her to go up them and then come down. Emerence refused, so Miss Dene brought her typing and sat typing there at the foot of the stairs most of the morning till Emerence gave in when we were halfway through Mittagessen and went up the stairs and then came down them again'. And how on earth anyone made any of that into *'cannibal'* is beyond me!" She concluded with another giggle in which everyone joined whole-heartedly and Hall rang with their peals of laughter.

"That old yarn!" Rosalie Dene said when they were all more or less sober again. "I'd nearly forgotten all about it myself. Trust you to remember, Mary-Lou!"

"What is the next torture you have in store for us?" "Bill" demanded.

"Well, it isn't Hallowe'en yet, but we thought *one* of the Hallowe'en games wouldn't be too bad," replied Madge Watson, the music prefect, who was responsible for it. "Bring those candles along, Lesley, will you? I've got the matches."

Lesley Malcolm dived behind the curtains which shut off the bottom of Hall and came out bearing an enormous tray on which stood twelve small candlesticks of the dinner-table variety, each with a gay candle in it. Madge lit the candles and then the two placed the candlsticks in a huge circle all round the room.

"Now," said Madge as she blew out her last match and dropped it on the tray. "You go round in turn, jumping over each candle. Every one that you leave alight represents a happy month for you. This one is November, seeing October is more than half over. Who'll begin?" She looked hopefully at the Staff.

"I will," Peggy Burnett said with a chuckle as she jumped up. "I don't in the least mind making a martyr of myself." She suddenly paused and looked at the two Heads with mischief in her eyes. "Do you remember the *first* time we ever tried this? It was in Tirol and that awful idiot Thelka had put on a frilly petticoat and nearly set herself on fire."

"Do I not!" "Bill" said with emphasis. "I don't often dislike my pupils, but *how* I disliked Thelka! But why are you raking up past history at a party? You go on and do your jumping." She cast a glance at Mlle de Lachennais and they both dissolved into giggles.

However, Peggy had gone to make her round and there was no one else likely to remind her that on that occasion, gay little Mlle had contrived to put out nine of the candles by landing heavily each time.

Peggy went lightly over every candle and when she had finished, the twelve tiny lights were still burning bravely. Miss Annersley followed and she hopped over them as lightly and sat down amid laughing applause from the girls Next came Miss Denny who took Handcrafts and such oddments as Italian and Spanish for those who wanted them. Now Miss Denny was a large, comfortable creature with very little spring in her. She set her feet together and jumped and landed with a thud which extinguished November completely. By the time she had made the round, not one candle remained alight. Everyone shrieked with laughter as she sat down, remarking affably, "Ah, well, I never was much of a jumper, even in my young days."

When every mistress had tried her luck, the prefects evidently considered that their guests had had long enough to rest. Madge skipped across to the piano while Elinor, Sybil, Lala and Bess hurriedly laid pairs of the long clay pipes known as "churchwardens" in crosses all round the room.

"I know that most people here know the Bacca Pipes jig," Hilary said from the dais. "Madge will play and you go on dancing till you break a pipe or send it flying."

At least half-a-dozen people cried off from this; but the rest did their best and Kathie, who had been a keen Folk Dancer at school, came off victor with her pipes still untouched when Biddy had sat down, having danced on to hers and left them in flinders. The girls cheered her and she went back to her seat, laughing and pink with pleasure and heat combined.

Elinor mounted the dais again. "Now there will be ten minutes' break to allow people to wash," she said simply. "Then we have supper."

The mistresses fled to their own special Splashery while the girls, who had seized the candle-jumping to go in turns to tidy themselves, remained in Hall and became very busy. When the last mistress returned to Hall, it was to find an elaborate supper-table drawn into the centre of the great room. The girls had switched off the lights, and down the centre of the table stood a procession of candles lighting up dishes of sandwiches and tiny rolls stuffed with meat; creams and jellies of all kinds; bowls of fruit salad; plates piled high with rosy apples and gleaming pears and, as a finishing touch, an enormous platter on which stood a castle modelled in strawberry ice-cream. This last, Sybil Russell had persuaded her aunt, Joey Maynard, to bring up from Interlaken that afternoon.

"All the work of our own fair hands," Blossom Willoughby explained as she offered her arm to Kathie, "—except the ice-cream, of course. Aunt Joey brought that from Interlaken. May I have the pleasure, Miss Ferrars?"

The prefects led the mistresses to the table and seated them ceremoniously. Then they served a delicious meal which, as Nancy murmured sotto voce to Rosalind Moore who sat next her, was more than welcome after all their recent exertions.

"I hope you girls are going to take pity on us after all this lavishness and let us down lightly immediately after," Miss Denny remarked to Elinor.

"Oh, yes; we thought of that," Elinor said with a laugh. "Do have a little more cream and jelly, Miss Denny. Or what about some of this concoction of Mary-Lou's?"

"I've only room for a little of that elegant ice-cream erection when you cut into it," Miss Denny said firmly. "Have mercy on my tummy, Elinor! It's not as young as yours!"

Supper over, Miss Annersley and Mlle excused themselves and went off to take Prayers for the rest of the school and dismiss the Juniors to bed. The various Matrons followed and Madge went back to the piano and initiated a brief singsong while the rest of the prefects tugged the table back behind the curtains where they could be heard quickly clearing it.

"I trust they will break nothing," Frau Mieders whispered to "Bill".

"They'll have to pay for it if they do and they've a few other uses for their pocket-money, especially with half-term so near," "Bill" returned cheerfully. "I wouldn't worry if I were you."

They were just finishing a rousing *Cockles and Mussels* when the Head and Mlle returned, followed a few minutes later by the Matrons. As if she had been waiting for this, Mary-Lou took the dais.

"This is *my* affair," she said in her usual bell-like tones. "The table will be brought back and on it are various articles. You will be given slips and pencils and will you please write down the use of each article. And *please* may we have the pencils back at the end."

Her imploring tone on this last sentence brought peals of laughter from everyone as four of the biggest prefects vanished behind the curtains and re-appeared, lugging the table with them. It was laden with a variety of articles and as soon as it came to rest, the Staff crowded round it while Hilary distributed slips of paper and pencils. Mary-Lou watched carefully and when everyone had been supplied, she looked at her watch and then said, "You may begin—*Now!*"

The prefects had certainly done their best to be confusing. Some things were easy enough to identify. An egg-whisk, a tin-opener and a hammer all went down on everyone's list. Others were not so easy and two or three beat everyone.

After ten minutes Mary-Lou said "Please correct your own and I'll read them out slowly."

Nancy Wilmot totted up her marks. "Well, with all the will in the world, I can't make it more than twenty-three. It doesn't speak well for me, does it?"

"Mines only eighteen," Joan Bertram announced sadly. "How many did you say there were, Mary-Lou?"

"Forty," Mary-Lou returned sweetly.

"Good gracious! Well, I'm well down on that one, at any rate."

In the end, the winner proved to be "Bill" with thirty-two to her credit, though she owned that one or two were wild guesses and it was more by good luck than good management that she had gained so many. Most of the others were in the twenties and Miss Denny mournfully announced *her* total as thirteen."

By this time. the evening was well advanced and Elinor, with an eye on the clock, called, "Last game! Will you all sit down, please, in pairs."

The mistresses found seats and the prefects hurriedly provided them with a folding table to each pair. Scissors, paste and pins were provided. Then Lala Winterton went the rounds and presented every mistress with two sheets of newspaper and a sheet of cardboard.

"But what, then, must we do with these?" Mlle demanded as she looked at hers.

Bess Appleton who was helping Lala, laughed. "This is Sybil's idea and she will explain in a minute."

Sybil Russell was already making her way to the dais. Kathie, sitting in the middle of the room, looked across at her and reflected that the Chalet School certainly had its fair share of pretty girls. Sybil, with her copper curls, violet eyes and perfect complexion allied to delicate features and a certain little air of dignity and grace that was quite unconscious, was as lovely a girl as you would find anywhere.

"Are you all ready?" she asked. "Well, then, this competition is to manufacture something out of your materials—and it may *not* be a paper boat. All paper boats are automatically disqualified. You have half-an-hour to do it in. I'm sorry we can't make it longer, but time's fugiting for all it's worth. Oh, and you must try to use as much of your materials as possible. Begin, please! "

"Oh, mercy me! " Kathie exclaimed as she surveyed her collection with dismay. "What on earth am I to do with this lot?"

"Well, I know what I'm doing with mine! " And Sharlie, who was sharing her table, began to cut her newspaper up into long, fine strips. "Paper beads! "

"But how will you string them?" Kathie asked.

"I'm going to demand needle and cotton, of course. And I'll cut the cardboard into stars and crosses to alternate with the beads." And Sharlie grabbed at Hilary who was going past and asked for a needle and cotton.

Miss Denny, as Handcrafts mistress, was not at a loss. She cut her cardboard into strips for frames and wove a set of paper dinner mats with strips of newspaper. The Head was busy with a marble rolling game, making her marbles of tightly wrapped newspaper and using the cardboard to form a board with a piece in which she cut openings pasted upright to one end. Someone else was reduced to paper fans with sticks of cardboard and making heavy weather of it. Someone else was cutting out birds and animals in newspaper and mounting them on the cardboard. Kathie heaved a deep sigh and set to work on a basket with a handle. As there was only one pot of paste to each couple, people got pasted by their partners more than once. Biddy o'Ryan was heard bemoaning the hardness of the cardboard as she cut through it and Miss Derwent shamelessly manufactured covers for blotters out of hers as the easiest thing she could think of. Matron went one better by cutting her cardboard into slips on each of which she printed a name with a pencil she produced from a pocket, declaring that she might as well make something useful of it and she needed a set of new slips for the linen room at Ste Thérèse's. On Elinor pointing out to her that she was not using her paper, she promptly turned it into two bags by pasting up the two sides and folding over one edge to cover the other which she had cut short.

At last Elinor called, "Time!" and the mistresses sat back while the prefects went the rounds, judging the results. Eventually, they decided that the best was a toy wheelbarrow made by Mlle Lenoir; Matron's was the most useful and Sharlie's necklace with its beads and alternate small stars and crosses the most decorative.

While Elinor was making this announcement, Mary-Lou and Blossom were carrying up to the top of the room a small table covered with a white cloth which was whisked off and behold! Prizes!

For the most part, the girls had contributed from their tuckboxes and slabs of chocolate and bags of sweets in cellophane wrappings were awarded; but Miss Denny got a booby prize of an enormous blue balloon and Kathie had a green one, as well as a set of Morris braces made of blue and scarlet braid, all hung with tiny bells for her

97

D

BACCA PIPES jig. "Bill" received a corkscrew and Mlle Lenoir a needlebook simply crammed with needles of all kinds.

When all the laughter and applause had ended, the Head stood up. "Thank you for a very delightful evening, girls," she said. "I know I'm speaking for all the Staff when I say that we have enjoyed ourselves thoroughly. And now," she went on in a rather different tone, "I don't know how everyone else feels, but I'm exhausted with laughter and all the awful things you've made us do. I'm for bed. Leave all the clearing up till tomorrow, Elinor, and run along to bed, all of you. I'm sure you must be as tired as we are!"

"Bill" took her place. "Before we go, though, I'm sure everyone would like to show the prefects how much we thank them for all the fun they've given us and all the thought and work they've put into tonight's entertainment Everyone—three cheers for the pre——"

"Not if I know it! And the Juniors all asleep—or if they're not, they ought to be!" Matron interrupted firmly. "Girls! We've cheered you! Now hurry up and go to bed and *be as quiet as you can!*"

She saw to it that they obeyed, for she waited until the last prefect was out of Hall and Miss Dene, who had waited with her, had locked the doors. Then she ushered the secretary upstairs where the prefects were already in their cubicles undressing, but glorying in the knowledge that their Evening had been a huge success. At the door of Matron's own room, Rosalie Dene paused to say good-night before she went to her own quarters in Miss Annersley's private suite.

"*Quite* as original as ever they've been, Matey," she said, with a low laugh.

"Oh, quite," Matron agreed, pausing with her hand on the door-handle. "Even." She opened it and prepared to fly, "to labelling you 'Cannibal' for the rest of their school careers!"

Chapter XII

WITH THE PREFECTS

HALF-TERM arrived and only a few of the girls went away this time. The rest stayed at school to take part in the various expeditions the authorities proposed for them. As there were so many, they were divided up into groups, sundry mistresses taking it in turn to be responsible for each group while the rest were free. As far as possible things were arranged to give each mistress at least two days to herself. As Miss Annersley remarked, it was *their* half-term as well.

Kathie was free on the Friday and Saturday, Sunday was the usual day of church and quiet walks. On Monday, she was scheduled to take a party of prefects to a little mountain resort much higher up, beyond even the Rösleinalp. They were to leave by the half-past eight train and would not return until the late afternoon. Wahlstein, the place where they were going, was the terminus of the line and her colleagues all assured her that she was in for a treat. The weather had changed and for the last three days, the sun had shone brightly and the skies were a clear, steadfast blue. Weather reports all said that it would continue for the next few days, so everyone looked forward to a good time.

"Though there's never any saying when the clouds will come down," Rosalie Dene had remarked when she gave Kathie her assignment. "Still, you have a reasonable prospect of a fine clear day."

"What is there to see—or do?" Kathie asked.

"Plenty! There's the glacier for one thing. I'd advise you to have your elevenses as soon as you get there and then set off for it at once. It's an hour's good going from the village—if you can call it a village," she added.

"Is it so very tiny, then?"

"Just the Gasthaus and half-a-dozen chalets. Hardly enough to call a hamlet. By the way, don't let the girls try to cross the glacier, will you? They say that the wet weather we had last week has made it unsafe unless you've got a guide with you. So forbid it if any of them show any desire to adventure. We don't want any accidents *this* Christmas term!"

"I should think not!" Kathie looked slightly alarmed. "They certainly won't go prancing about on the ice if *I* can prevent it. Looking at it will have to do them."

"Oh, it will. They'll be well and truly warned before you set out that that's all they may do. When they've satisfied their curiosity—I hope you're prepared to answer a whole volley of questions!—you can come down again and go to the Gasthaus for Mittagessen. I've arranged all that and they're expecting you. Then there's a little glacier lake at the other end of the shelf—rather lovely, too. You can take them to see it and mercifully, no one is likely to want even to paddle. That lake is icy on the hottest day. I know for I've tried it." Rosalie paused to laugh. "Talk about stinging! That water stings you up with a vengeance! Leave yourselves time for Kaffee und Kuchen at the Gasthaus and remember that the train always leaves dead on time. It's the railway terminus, by the way."

"Supposing it *should* come on to rain?" Kathie asked. "Should I bring the girls straight back?"

"That will depend on yourself. They have a big room at the Gasthaus where they can dance and there's a tiny museum where they show examples of woodcarving and lace and embroideries and so on. You please yourself what you do."

There the instructions ended, except that Kathie was warned that the girls were to take no risks with casting off any garments. The air would be icy and no one wanted to begin the second half of the term with pneumonia or pleurisy cases.

Rosalie had given the new mistress all this information on Sunday afternoon, adding that Frühstück would be ready for her party and two others who were off to Berne and Lucerne respectively, at half-past seven next morning and everyone must be ready to leave the school by eight.

The mistress came down to Frühstück next morning to find only three tables occupied, for the rest had an extra hour's bed as they were not going far. Her own party were at the prefects' table, nine in number. They were headed by Elinor Pennell and her great friend, Blossom

Willoughby. Besides them there were Sybil Russell, Madge Watson, Hilary Bennet, Lesley Malcolm, Bess Appleton, Lala Winterton and Mary-Lou Trelawney. They were all in their climbing-kit of blue suits with dull crimson trimming and silver buttons and their berets and mitts lay beside them on the table.

Warned by Biddy o'Ryan, Kathie herself had donned her new climbing-kit—for the first time, since so far excursions had had to be few and far between, thanks to the weather, and all of them had been down to the valley. She had never worn such a thing before and she felt very self-conscious as she entered the big Speisesaal where Elinor Pennel drew out her chair and Mary-Lou went to bring her coffee.

"We always feed together on expedition mornings," Elinor explained as she gave the mistress a bowl of smoking hot porridge. "Make a good meal, Miss Ferrars. You'll need it with all this scrambling and climbing we have before us. Will you have eggs after? Run and tell Karen eggs for Miss Ferrars, will you, Lesley?"

Lesley went to the buttery hatch to give the message while Mary-Lou arrived with the huge cup of milky coffee. Kathie smiled her thanks at the girl as it was set down at her place and then set to work to clear her bowl of porridge and cream before beginning on the generous plateful of scrambled eggs Lesley brought her. She had been told the evening before to eat a good meal as reaching the glacier meant a bit of a tussle and they would have the walk to the Gasthaus first and that was a matter of twenty minutes or so.

"It's not that it's so far away," Sharlie Andrews had told her, "so much as that it's over the most awful ground. In fact it's one gaudy scramble the whole way, once you leave the train. People used to go up to visit the lake as well as to see the glacier or climb the peak. The lake's not far from the railway, but there's only one clump of pines up there so they had to build the Gasthaus among them and that's the glacier end, anyhow."

"I suppose the pines help to break the force of winter storms?" Kathie said.

"Not only that. They make any odd avalanches scatter instead of hurtling down with one fell swoop," put in Nancy Wilmot who was sitting near. "Not that *you* have any need to worry. That will come next term when the

101

spring's behind the door and the Föhn blows and there are scatters of light new snow. *This* isn't avalanche time, my child."

"I should hope not!" Kathie had exclaimed with fervour.

No one talked much at Frühstück, she found. Everyone was intent on finishing her meal and getting off for her train. A few remarks went round, but for the most part everyone concentrated on stoking up, to quote Peggy Burnett who was in charge of the Berne party with Nancy Wilmot as assistant, since they were taking the entire Upper IV and it needed at least two people to keep an eye on those young persons.

As soon as her table was finished, Kathie stood up and marched them off.

"I'll meet you outside in five minutes," she remarked as she fled to pull on the green cap matching her suit over her smooth brown hair, settle her knapsack on her shoulders and plunge her hands into her mitts. She picked up her alpenstock, cast a final look at herself into the bureau mirror and then raced downstairs and out into the path behind the Splasheries where she found her group waiting for her. Very trim and alert they all looked and as soon as she appeared, they closed round her in an eager bunch.

"Can we get off now, Miss Ferrars?" Blossom cried. "We shan't have any too much time for the train and they hate us if we keep them waiting!"

"Yes; line up in pairs," Kathie said. "Are you all sure you've got everything you want? Then lead on, Elinor and Blossom."

Dark-eyed Elinor and Blossom, fair and lovely with her perfect features and complexion and golden curls, led the way and the rest paired off and followed them, Mary-Lou and Hilary being the tail. They marched briskly down the road to the station and arrived just as the sounds of the rack-and-pinion train coming up to them were heard. Then it arrived and they poured in just as Miss Burnett and Miss Wilmot reached the school side of the tiny station with their mob of excited Middles. The prefects waved and the Middles waved back. Then they were off, climbing up and up. Past Mahlhausen and the Rösleinalp and Blumenthal and all the other tiny hamlets they went, passing the down train just after Mahlhausen. At last the train came to a stop before a platform built on the edge of a grassy stretch where they stepped out and through the little turnstile. They had arrived a Wahlstein!

"What a queer, sourish smell!" Kathie exclaimed as she joined her charges after a hurried look round the carriage to make sure that nothing had been left behind.

"The glacier ice," Mary-Lou who was nearest, replied. "But isn't the air fresh and *clean* up here! It makes you feel as if you'd just come out of a cold tub and got into fresh clothes." And she swallowed several mouthfuls of the thin, pure air.

"Our latest example of a stranded codfish!" said Blossom with a grin. "Come off it, Mary-Lou! All the same, it does buck you up," she added as she sniffed loudly.

Elinor had been looking round. "Miss Ferrars, turn round and look straight ahead of you," she said urgently.

Kathie obligingly turned round. A gasp of amazement broke from her at the panorama she saw before her. Line after line of mighty crests rose, one behind the other, all gleaming silver in the late October sunlight, all soaring up to the blue autumn sky with a dignity and austere beauty that robbed the mistress of any words.

"How wonderful!" she breathed at last. "It's one of the most marvellous sights I ever saw!"

" 'I will lift up mine eyes unto the hills'," said a voice behind her in low tones.

Kathie turned back to see Mary-Lou go vividly pink and remark hurriedly to Hilary, "Oh, I know David and the rest of the Israelites were really terrified of the hills because of the bandits that hid there and that he never meant that his help came from them. All the same, that's how it always strikes me whenever I see them like this. It—somehow it makes me *realise* God more."

Hilary, whose face had been sparkling with mischief, grew serious as she replied, "I know what you mean. When you see wonders like this you do begin to feel how immense He is to create such a world." She turned to Kathie to say in the same grave voice, "It does, doesn't it. Miss Ferrars?"

"Yes," Kathie said thoughtfully. She gave the two girls a keen look. So far, her duties had given her little chance of seeing much of the prefects and she had had no idea that they could be as serious as this. In her own prefect days, she and her friends had never discussed such things, preferring to skim over the surface. Plainly the Chalet School encouraged its girls to go deep. Her pondering was broken into by a quite different type of remark.

"Well," observed Lala Winterton, "fine views are all very well, but *I* should like my elevenses. This air may make you feel clean all right, but it does zip up your appetite. I'm ravenous! "

"Lala, you Goth! " Elinor exclaimed, laughing. "Trust you to bring us all off our perches and down to earth again."

"It's all very well for you folk who have imaginations," Lala said stolidly. "No one ever yet accused me of being anything but matter of fact. And if I may remind you all, time's slipping by and we've got to get to the glacier after we've had our coffee and whatever they supply in the way of buns or biscuits. Don't you agree we ought to go on, Miss Ferrars?"

Kathie laughed as she looked at the pleasant-faced, red-haired girl who was clearly little given to musings. "I suppose it's just as well to have matter of fact people with us as well as the other kind, Lala. Some of us would never keep our feet on the ground, but for them. Very well; we'll leave this for the time being. Come along, girls! We've yet to find our Gasthaus and introduce ourselves."

"Not much difficulty in that," Mary-Lou said cheerfully as she turned away after a last look. "It's straight ahead. We go on till we come to it. Oh, by the way, Miss Ferrars," her natural eagerness had overcome the diffidence Kathie's obvious dislike of her had engendered, "did you know that we've come halfway round the mountain? Those giants lie south of us. The line turns all the way, you know, and goes round. Over there, far away behind those mountains, is Italy."

"Really?" Kathie exclaimed in surprise. "I'd no idea of that."

"Well, I only knew it this summer when we came up here with a party," Mary-Lou owned with a grin. "I found it out then, though and it was a shock. I'd always thought that the line went straight up. Anyhow," she beamed benignantly round on the whole party, "I thought you'd all like to know."

"I didn't notice it," Sybil Russell confessed. "I did rather wonder when I saw all those giant peaks, but I

104

thought perhaps we hadn't seen them before because the Platz lies so much lower and we've never been up here till now."

"Oh, Sybs! You know we run down to the valley on our side," Mary-Lou reminded her. "Not," she added, "that it's ever what you could call really flat. But it's to the south that you get all those masses."

They stopped talking after that and made their way along the shelf to the Gasthaus. As Mary-Lou had said, it was easy enough to find. The difficulty lay in getting there. The ground was rough and uneven in the extreme and strewn with great boulders round which they had to walk. They mounted little ridges and descended little dips the whole way, too. Anything like the plateau of their own shelf wasn't to be found. The actual distance was not much more than half a mile; but by the time they had reached the clump of black-trunked pine trees which clustered round the building on three sides, everyone was boiling hot and one or two people begged leave to throw open their windcheaters. Thanks to Rosalie's warning, Kathie was too wise to allow it. They might be hot, but the wind up here was fresh with a distinct nip in it. She made them go on as they were, though she let them take off mitts and berets which helped a little.

Frau Elsner of the Gasthaus was on the look-out for them and as they toiled along between the trees, eyes on the look-out for spreading roots, she appeared on the balcony that ran across the front of the palace and waved vigorously to them.

"I hope," said Elinor apprehensively as she waved back, "that she can speak ordinary German. If it's patois, I've had it!"

"Oh, she'll speak all right," Blossom said easily. "These hotel-keepers all are the most marvellous linguists."

"Do people ever come up here to stay?" Kathie asked as they left the trees at last and walked across the one comparatively flat stretch they had yet met.

"Probably anyone who wants to climb to the summit of the mountain," Mary-Lou said. "They start early in the morning, about four or five, you know, and it would be easier from here."

She had to stop there for they had reached the Gasthaus and Frau Elsner was welcoming them in very fair German, but with a broader accent than most of them knew. She bade them welcome and ushered them into the Speisesaal where one of the long tables was laid with big cups and plates piled high with buns and bread-twists and dishes of ivory butter. She saw them seated and hurried out to bring the coffee-urn. She returned bearing a great urn and followed by a little girl of eight whose long flaxen hair swung in two pigtails below her waist. She carried an enormous jug which contained hot milk and she smiled shyly at the girls as she put it on the table beside the urn. Mary-Lou, always friendly, spoke the few words of patois she knew, but the child coloured and hid behind her mother.

Kathie dispensed the coffee and when they were all busy with the good fare provided, Mary-Lou heaved a gusty sigh and remarked, "There are times when I could *bite* Uncle Jack for having me shaven and shorn last year! I'm bound to say though, it takes me next to no time to do my hair nowadays."

Twenty minutes later, they had finished and after telling Frau Elsner that they hoped to be back for noon Mittagessen, they set off again.

As Sharlie had told Kathie, the path became increasingly hard. It was not really difficult, but they were mounting all the time and the footing was uneven in the extreme. Kathie sent Mary-Lou to the head of the party as she had been there before and might be supposed to have some idea of the way. She herself went to the tail. While they were among the trees, they had to go in Indian file. Then they came out and, for a few hundred yards, were able to proceed in a body. After that they struck the path to the glacier and here, Mary-Lou halted them.

"I think we ought to put on our coloured glasses before we go much further," she said. "We've had rain at the Platz, but up here, it's probably been snow and if there's fresh snow on the glacier, it'll be dazzling with this bright sun. No one wants an attack of snow blindness."

"What exactly *is* snow blindness?" the mistress asked as they fished in their knapsacks for the coloured glasses Matron had insisted on their bringing with them.

"I don't know from my own experience," Bess said, "but Emerence Hope let herself in for an attack last year. She said it was horrible. Everything looks swimmy and a sort of blood-red mist is over everything. It only lasted a day or two with her, but a really bad attack can go on for

106

a while. It's caused by the glare from the snow on a sunny day."

Kathie hurriedly put on her glasses. "I should hate to have an attack!"

"We all would. Thank goodness Mary-Lou remembered about the glasses in time," Bess said as she settled hers on her nose. "I'd forgotten all about it."

They set off again in pairs, but it was toilsome work and before long, Lala was complaining of feeling boiled again and Sybil informed Madge Watson that her legs were aching madly.

In the clear thin air, her voice carried and Mary-Lou who had been going at a steady pace, paused to look down on the long string tagging after her and say in her usual bell-like tones, "Bend your knees as you step, all of you! That'll save your poor shins quite a lot. You can't walk straight-legged in the mountains. Bend just a trifle with every step. *Now* are you all right?"

Her tone was slightly offhand, though she did not mean it and did not realise it, and Kathie instantly stiffened up mentally. Really, Mary-Lou seemed to forget that she was addressing a mistress with her fellow-prefects. It was high time someone told her that was no way to behave! Foolishly, she paid no heed to the advice and before long, her legs were aching as badly as Sybil's which did not improve her temper, though she said nothing about it and went on doggedly.

Up and up they toiled and, at long last, a cry from Hilary told her that the end was in sight. Setting her teeth, she struggled up the last bit of the stony road and came out with the rest on to a great flat rock. Before them stretched the glacier, dazzling with its blues and greens and patches of white snow here and there. The sour smell she had noticed on first reaching Wahlstein was all about them. They had arrived!

Chapter XIII

A Narrow Shave!

"This," said Blossom, breaking the silence that had fallen on all of them at first sight of the glacier, "really *is* something! I know, of course, that a glacier isn't just a smooth flow of ice like a flow of frozen water. At least that isn't what I mean, but you all understand. In my *mind* I knew it was just chunks of ice all crammed together—"

"But that's just what they're not!" Lala interrupted her. "Look at the great crack over there—crevasse, I suppose I should say—and there's another. And that huge one running zigzag across the middle! They're certainly not crammed together."

"I was speaking," Blossom reminded her with immense dignity.

Lala made an impish face at her. "Continue, oh, Queen! Pour forth to us the benefits of your words of wisdom!"

Blossom forgot her dignity and grimaced back at her friend with a will. For such a remarkably pretty girl, she could turn herself into something calculated, as Mary-Lou remarked in a detached voice, to scare a horse from his oats. Even Kathie laughed when she saw it and Sybil Russell gently suggested that if Blossom went on making faces like that, she would stick that way, some day.

"Not much fear!" retorted the games prefect complacently. "I'm like my Aunt Con who is the best hand at making faces that ever I knew. At school, so Aunt José informed me, she was known as 'India-rubber Gob' in her young days!"

"Never mind that. You go on and tell us what you were about to say when Lala barged in on you," Hilary said.

"Can't! It's gone now!" was the laconic reply. "Anyway, I don't suppose it was anything of real importance. Miss Ferrars, is this thing *really* moving? To me it looks literally frozen stiff and solid and quite immovable."

"What I'd like to know," said Madge Wilson, a quiet

girl who usually had little to say, "is what on earth are all the weird moans and groans coming from it?"

"It really is moving," Kathie said. "Those very sounds are caused by the movement. But you're quite right, Madge. They *are* weird."

"I shouldn't like to be here alone in the middle of the night," Elinor observed. "It's much too eerie for my liking! "

"How fast does a glacier move, Miss Ferrars?" Mary-Lou asked.

"It varies," Kathie replied coldly. "Naturally when one is coming down a steep descent it moves at a somewhat faster rate than one which is on only a gentle slope. That is a matter of common sense, Mary-Lou."

Mary-Lou completely innocent of having offended her, looked at her with widened eyes for she could *not* account for this chilliness and formality. She had the wisdom, however, to reply merely, "I see. Thank you, Miss Ferrars."

"I once heard," said Lala who, with a journalist father, had a trick of coming out with totally unexpected pieces of information, "that a couple were honeymooning in the Alps and the husband broke his neck down a crevasse in some glacier and was lost as they couldn't get at the body. The guides told the bride that at the end of thirty years it might be recovered at the end, so she made her home in Switzerland and waited for it. Of course, she grew older as the years went on and when they were up, she went to where the stream leaves the ice and presently the body came through. It was the body of a young man in the twenties, but she, who had waited all these years, was a middle-aged woman in the fifties with grey hair and wrinkles."

"How simply *horrible!* " Lesley Malcolm exclaimed. "Poor thing! What an awful tragedy for her! "

"What happened to her, Lala?" Bess asked.

"I never heard. They buried him in the nearest village, but whether she went on living in Switzerland or whether she went back to England when it was all over, I just couldn't tell you," Lala replied. "Dad didn't say."

"It was dreadful for her," Sybil said, "but I think it would have been better if she had gone back to England and got some work to do. Isn't just living round, waiting for his body to come, what they call 'feeding your sorrow?' I don't think that's right. Far better find a job and go at it."

Mary-Lou looked at her. "Do you know, it was an awful shock of course, but I think she'd got over that, seeing him as she remembered him, young and—and fresh, sort of, may have been a comfort to her. She never had to see him growing old along with her, nor his face lined with worry and his hair going grey, perhaps even *bald*! And she has a memory of him which would last her all the rest of her life. She might have had to wait till she died to see him again as he was and now he would always be young to her."

Kathie glanced at her, wondering about this girl with her offhand manner and her habit of going so deeply into things. What a curious contradiction she was!

"I hadn't thought of it that way," Lesley said thoughtfully. "I shouldn't be surprised if you were right, though."

"Oh, well, it all happened years and years and years ago," Lala said cheerfully. "Dad said it was before the first World War. I expect she's dead now and with him for keeps, so it won't matter to her. May we walk a little way along the bank, Miss Ferrars, and get a good view of the glacier?"

Thinking they had had enough of the somewhat morbid topic, Kathie assented and they began a fine scramble among the moraine rocks which effectually turned their minds away from Lala's story. They knew, of course, that the lateral moraines were built up with boulders and landslides from the mountain caused by the action of the ice, undercutting the ground as it ground its way down the mountain side. But they had never seen the result with their own eyes before and they were greatly impressed. Two or three of them exclaimed over the size of the huge boulders to be seen perched among the ice pinnacles.

"Well, look over there to the other side," Kathie said, pointing to a veritable grandfather among rocks. "See that huge thing over there? It'll be swept up against the side some time and help to make the moraine over there."

Elinor shaded her eyes with her hand to look. "When will that happen? Won't it just go straight on with the ice? It seems to have fallen quite a little way out."

"When a spur of the mountain causes the glacier to curve round," Kathie replied.

"Don't glaciers shrink sometimes?" the Head Girl asked as she stepped back.

"Of course they do!" cried Mary-Lou, butting in in her own inimitable way. "Think of the huge one that used to cover almost the whole of North America. And there was another over most of the British Isles and what's now the North Sea and on into Europe during the Ice Age. They've both gone now. Oh, and they come on again."

"How d'you know that?" Blossom asked instantly.

"By Greenland," Mary-Lou replied. She proceeded to mark her point. "Don't you remember when the Vikings first found it, it was a *green* land and they planted farms there which did well. But from all I've ever heard or read there's no farming of that kind done there now. Practically the whole island is a glacier."

"Yes; and didn't they call the shores of the St. Lawrence Vinland because they could grow grapes there?" Madge chimed in. "Miss Ferrars, do you think the Ice Age may be coming back, perhaps? For I don't think you can grow grapes there outside nowadays—or can you?"

"You *would* think of a nasty crack like that one!" slangy Blossom said. "She isn't right, is she, Miss Ferrars?"

"Well," Kathie said, "there *is* a theory that what we call the Ice Age isn't by any means the first one this planet has known, nor likely to be the last, either. According to some geographers, we are slowly returning to *an* Ice Age. But it won't come in your time, so don't worry, Blossom."

"Do *you* think it's true?" Blossom asked with flattering eagerness.

"I can't tell you for I don't know. I've never studied it in any detail. But it's true enough that the northern ice has advanced towards the Equator since the days of the Norsemen. So much has been proved—as Mary-Lou told you just now."

The girls were suitably impressed by this and for some minutes they discussed it. Kathie was nearly overwhelmed by the questions they poured over her. Finally she broke away, laughing as she cried, "This is a holiday—mine as well as yours! I'm giving no extra geography lessons just now. Not if *I* know it! You'll wait till Miss Moore takes you again and ask *her*."

"I will," Hilary said with a wicked look in her very blue eyes. "I'm most interested and I'd like to know."

"In the meantime, we've gone far enough up the glacier,"

111

Kathie said, wondering to herself just *how* Rosalind Moore would take her revenge for this result of their expedition. "It really is time we were thinking of turning back. Look at the time! It's after eleven and we told Frau Elsner we'd be back at the Gasthaus for midday lunch! You leave geography alone and come along back, all of you!"

"Be careful not to go too near the edge, girls!" Kathie called rather anxiously. "I should think after last week's weather the ground will be extremely friable—Hilary! Go round *behind* that spur! You can't possibly go outside it! Don't be so foolhardy, please!"

Hilary grimaced at Mary-Lou who was with her, but luckily, the mistress did not see it and the girl was obedient enough, especially when her friend said in an undertone, "Hilary, you *ass!* You don't want to land in the nearest crevasse, do you—or even on an ice pinnacle?" she added as Hilary went ahead of her through the narrow cleft between the spur and the mountain.

Laughing and chattering as they went, the party made its way with many exclamations and a good deal of rough scrambling towards the head of the path up which they had come to the glacier. Thanks to their nailed boots and their alpenstocks, they were able to keep their feet, but they were all beginning to tire and when they reached the path at last, more than one person was grateful to Elinor when she called back to know if they might pause for one last look at the glacier.

They were divided up into four groups by this time, Elinor and Blossom with Madge and Sybil had reached the head of the path. Lala, Lesley and Bess were a little further back, but not very far. Mary-Lou and Hilary were behind them. Last of all was Kathie herself, standing at the moment on an enormous slab of rock that overhung the glacier and gave a wonderful view of it. They all halted and gazed at the desolate mass of ice pinnacles and crevasses with here and there frail bridges of snow gleaming with a dazzling whiteness in the sunshine of the autumn morning.

Kathie was absorbed in the scene before her. It was her first glacier and she was deeply impressed by it. Most of the others were as absorbed as she was. Only Mary-Lou, moved by some feeling she could never explain either then or later, glanced away at the mistress and her perch. There was a bare two yards between Kathie and the two

112

prefects and, with a sudden yell that startled everyone, Mary-Lou leaped back, grabbed Miss Ferrars by the right arm and literally hauled her back off the slab with a force and swiftness that nearly swept Kathie off her feet.

She was furious. "How *dare* you?" she began. But even as she spoke the first word it was frozen on her lips for, as if it had been sliced out of the solid mountain by a gigantic invisible knife, the enormous mass swayed, heaved, and then broke completely away, crashing down on to the glacier where it was shattered into a thousand pieces, some scattering far and wide on the ice, some vanishing down crevasses.

The girls screamed with one voice, but Kathie herself stood rigid. Three inches and no more lay between herself and the appalling gash in the earth. Mary-Lou, white as a sheet, still gripped her arm firmly and Hilary, quick to see what was needed, had clutched Mary-Lou's other arm and flung her own free one round a jut of rock that rose just there. Between them they contrived to drag the mistress back into safety before the thunderous echoes of the fall had even died away.

Kathie simply went. For the moment, she felt almost paralysed. Mary-Lou got her round Hilary's rock before she slackened her hold. Hilary, nearly as white as her friend, stepped forward and slung a supporting arm round the young mistress and Kathie, slowly reviving from the shock, was thankful for it. Then as Hilary drew her closer, she came back to life again and, with a violent effort, managed to pull herself together. She gently released herself from the hold of the two girls and looked anxiously towards where the rest were standing, silent now that they realised that the worst had *not* happened, though Sybil was sobbing and Madge was not far from it.

"Are—are you all quite safe?" Kathie gasped in quavering tones.

"Quite safe!" Elinor replied in what was meant to be a reassuring voice, though every word trembled. "Oh, Miss Ferrars, are you all right?"

"Yes, thank you." Kathie was recovering herself now. She turned to Mary-Lou and Hilary. "I owe my life to you two, especially Mary-Lou. Thank you more than I can say. But Mary-Lou, how did you know that that slab was—" She stopped short. Full understanding of her escape had come and she felt suddenly sick.

"I don't know," Mary-Lou faltered. She, too, was badly affected and, apart from that, her back felt nearly as bad as it had done when she first came round after the bad accident of nearly a year ago. "I—I think—I just—felt it, somehow."

Lala came to the rescue. True to her matter-of-fact nature, she was less upset than the others just then. As Blossom remarked much later on, there were times when it was just as well to lack much imagination.

"Look here!" she said abruptly. "It's all been pretty nasty, but it's over now. What we want is a hot drink and some food to help us pull ourselves together. I vote we get on back to the Gasthaus. We can discuss the whole thing there after we've had something to eat. Mary-Lou, you look pretty sick. Have you ricked your back again by any chance?"

Kathie swung round and saw the girl was still greenish-white with no colour in her lips. "Did you hurt yourself, dragging me out of the way like that?" she asked anxiously as, forgetting the fact that one arm felt as if it had been wrenched out of its socket, she went swiftly to Mary-Lou. "Can you manage to get past this jag of rock?" She passed the good arm cautiously round Mary-Lou, holding her gently but firmly under the shoulders. "This will help—oh, we can't do it this way yet! Try to go a few steps forward, Mary-Lou! Girls! You, Blossom, and you, Bess, come and make a queen's chair for Mary-Lou once she's past the jag. We must get her back to the Gasthaus as soon as possible."

"I'm all right," Mary-Lou said pluckily. She took a cautious step forward and then another and another and was round and out on the open path. "There, I've done it. No one could manage a queen's chair up here, Miss Ferrars. There just isn't room, though it's awfully decent of you to think of it. But it can't be done. I can manage on my own arched insteps, anyway. Blossom or someone can give me an arm in the wider places though, and we'll get on faster. But there's nothing wrong, really. I just felt the old bruise for a moment or two."

All the same, she was white to the lips and Kathie felt anxious about her. The girls said nothing then, but they were equally anxious about the mistress. She was almost as white as Mary-Lou and when she moved, her wrenched arm was torture, though she only bit her lips and went on behind Hilary who, as she afterwards confessed, fully expected to find herself between two swooning females at any moment!

Blossom gave Mary-Lou an arm wherever she could down the steep path. All heaved sighs of relief when at last they left the path and reached the rough turf of the shelf proper, though there were still the pines to negotiate.

When they were safely there, Kathie reasserted her authority. Mary-Lou was clearly in pain and she insisted that the girl should be carried to the Gasthaus where she could lie down and rest the weak back. Mary-Lou pulled a face over it, but she had the sense to make no demur which was as well, for Kathie herself felt nearer to fainting than she had ever done in her life before and could have endured nothing extra. Lala and Blossom made a queen's chair and she sat on their clasped hands and submitted to being carried to the pinewoods. But when they came to the edge of the clearing where the Gasthaus stood, Mary-Lou insisted on being set down.

"You know what these people can be like," she said to the rest of the party. "Frau Elsner will go off like a hundred squibs at once! I wouldn't put it past her to ring up the school and make a horror story out of it and there's no need for that. Please. Miss Ferrars, the aching is easier—it honestly is. I'll rest when we get there if you want me to, but do let me walk the rest now."

Kathie gave her a sharp look, but the colour had returned to her lips though she was still white. She herself felt incapable of any argument just then, so she agreed. "Very well. But be careful how you go, Mary-Lou. Don't trip up or Matron may pack you off to bed for a fortnight when you get back."

Elinor and Sybil, now recovered from her sobs, closed up round the mistress and they set off on the last part of the walk. It was only a few steps, but by the time they had reached the Gasthaus where Frau Elsner was on the lookout for them, both Kathie and Mary-Lou felt that they had reached the end of their tethers. They were thankful to sink down on the hard benches and rest their weary bones while the hostess bustled off to return with a trayful of smoking hot soup, very strong and delicious, which cheered up the invalids and ended any fear of their fainting away. By the time they had also finished platefuls of stuffed veal with buttered potatoes and French beans in a delicate sauce, followed by enormous pancakes filled with boiling jam sauce, everyone looked much more like herself. Mary-Lou stated that her back was not aching nearly so much and the pain in Kathie's arm had been subdued to a dull ache that was bearable if trying. Coffee topped up the meal.

"What about going back by the next train?" Elinor asked after the first mouthful or two.

An outcry from Mary-Lou answered her. "What on earth *for*? I thought we were going to see the lake, too. Miss Ferrars, do you feel as if you'd rather take us all straight back? For if anyone's thinking of my silly back, there's no need. The pain's nearly gone and I can walk quite well."

"I was only thinking perhaps you and Miss Ferrars ought to lie down on your beds and rest after this morning's adventure," Elinor said.

Kathie shuddered. Rest on her bed was the last thing she wanted just then. She was much too afraid that she would have nightmares if she went to sleep.

"If you're sure it won't hurt your back, Mary-Lou, I think perhaps we had better stick to our original plans," she said. "It would give the Heads an awful shock if they saw us coming back a couple of hours or so before we need. The lake is quite near the station. I propose that we sit quietly here for a while and then go and see it and to the station from there. Don't you want to see the museum, girls? Mary-Lou and I can rest while you visit it. She looked questioningly at the girl and Mary-Lou nodded.

"That's a jolly good idea! But before we break up the party, I'd like to say something. Please, everyone, lets keep all this affair quiet from the rest of the school. Oh, not the Heads, idiot! " as Lala exclaimed. "I know *they've* got to be told. But don't, I implore you, broadcast it among the kids. It's no business of theirs and Hilary and I would rather you didn't. Isn't that so, Hilary?"

Hilary nodded. "It is," she said with decision.

Kathie hesitated. "I shall go to Miss Annersley as soon as we get in," she said finally. "As for the others knowing about it, I'll leave that to you people to decide. If Mary-Lou and Hilary would rather nothing was said, perhaps we ought to agree, though I'd like everyone to know how quick and clear-headed both of them were," she added.

116

"*I* don't want to talk about it," Sybil said with a shudder. She was highly-strung and had had a bad shock. "I vote we do as they say and keep it dark."

"Well, as Mary-Lou points out, it's no business of the kids," Bess agreed.

"So long as the Heads know—and Matey, for she'd better have a look at Miss Ferrar's arm and Mary-Lou's back in case they've done any real damage—I quite agree," Elinor said.

So it was decided. The girls went off to look at the museum and buy one or two oddments of lace and wood-carving while the two invalids rested in a silence that was oddly companionable. Then they said goodbye to the Gasthaus and made their slow way to the lake which was well worth seeing as it lay in its deep cleft, pure jade green, gleaming under the sun. After that, they made for the train and finally reached the school where the prefects went off to change and Kathie, very weary between strain and pain, went slowly to the Head's drawing-room where she found both of them having Kaffee und Kuchen with Joey Maynard who was looking excited.

Kathie had been dreading telling her story, but she never got a chance just then. As she closed the door behind her, Joey leapt up from her chair.

"Oh, good! Here's someone else I can tell! "

"Joey, do sit down and be sensible!" Miss Annersley said, laughing.

"Sensible! And me with such news! Sensible yourself, Hilda Annersley! Kathie! *What* do you think is the very latest?"

Kathie gaped at her, blinking like an owl. Joey paused to gather herself together. Then in a voice that simply clanged with triumph, she announced, "I'm a great-aunt —by marriage! My niece-by-marriage, Daisy Rosomon, had a son early this morning! How's *that* for news?"

Chapter XIV

A NICE PROSPECT!

THANKS to Joey's spectacular methods, the glacier affair, as the prefects christened it, tended to sink into the background after that. Kathie and Mary-Lou had to interview Matron who took them in hand with her accustomed thoroughness.

"Hot baths for you two," she said firmly. "I'll touch you both up with my own lotion afterwards. No; I won't insist on bed, Mary-Lou, so take that glum look off your face. You'll be all the better for easing your mind with a little mild gossip. But I think *early* bed might be a good thing. What about you, my dear?" She turned to Kathie. "Would you like to go to bed now?"

"Oh, *no*!" Kathie replied with fervour. "I'd *much* rather be in the middle of things, thank you, Matron. But a hot bath sounds rather good," she added wearily.

Matron regarded her thoughtfully. Then she nodded. "Very well. Off you go to the bathroom. I'll bring you some of my special bath crystals and they'll help to relieve your aching. I'll bring you some, too, Mary-Lou. You'll both feel better after a good bath and a change into fresh clothes."

But when the pair had departed to obey her, she turned to the two Heads. "That girl is too imaginative," she said seriously. "I'm going to give her a good sedative tonight." With which she left the room to see about the crystals and the lotion.

"You'd better wear a sling for a day or two," she said when she had finished dabbing the lotion on Kathie's arm. "You must have given the muscles a nasty wrench and you'll feel it for the next few days. I'll give you something to make you sleep," Matron said thoughtfully.

She had also seen the rest of the party, but most of them were recovering quickly and she saw no need to dose them. Hilary admitted to feeling tired, and Elinor and Sybil were ordered to report in her room at bedtime for a mild sedative, but that was all. In any case, Joey insisted on giving her news to the school at large and the excitement it aroused went far to turning the girls' minds to pleasant things. All the elder ones had known Daisy Rosomon in the days when she was Daisy Venables and a much-loved Head Girl and they were thrilled to hear of the arrival of her son.

Kathie sat quietly. She was feeling very glad that she had tomorrow in which to rest and pull herself together. Her arm was throbbing and she also had a bad headache. Miss Annersley, passing her, saw her face and stopped.

"Kathie, I'm afraid you're feeling all in," she said anxiously.

Kathie lifted her heavy eyes with a faint smile. "It's just my arm's aching rather a little and now my silly head's started." She said.

"I don't wonder," the Head said promptly. "You've had a very nasty experience. I'm more sorry than I can say that it happened. What about going to bed now? You can slip away quite easily. The girls won't notice and Matron will give you something to help you. Come along! "

Kathie felt too poorly to argue. She obeyed meekly and Miss Annersley saw her upstairs and into Matron's hands.

That lady gave her one look and then ordered her to bed. "I'll come and dab your arm again," she said, "and bring something to help you to sleep."

Kathie undressed and when Matron arrived, she was in bed. The school's beloved tyrant anointed the poor arm again and then produced a hot drink.

"Down with it! " she commanded. "Drain it to the last drop and no arguments! "

Twenty minutes after Kathie had been tucked up and left alone in the dark room, she was in a deep dreamless sleep from which she never roused for twelve solid hours when she was awakened by someone coming in and pulling her curtains open.

"Well?" demanded Matron. "Feeling better? Sit up and I'll give you a sponge and towel and you can sponge your face. Then breakfast! "

Yawning and still half asleep, Kathie did as she was told and finally had a tempting tray laid across her knees and discovered that not only was her head better, but she was hungry.

"I've had such a beautiful sleep," she said as Matron

119

poured out her coffee. "But how silent the place is! What ever time is it?"

"After nine—and, of course, it's silent," Matron returned. "The girls are all off on the final trip of the holiday. You've slept the clock round and you look a different creature, let me tell you! Such a washed-out looking object as *you* were last night I never wish to see again! Eat your egg! It's beautifully boiled. I did it myself."

Of all things, Kathie hated a lightly boiled egg, but she dared not say anything. She set to work and presently the plates were cleared and the gay little coffee-pot and matching milk jug empty.

"Now," said Matron as she rose to take the tray. "You may stay where you are till eleven. If you like to get up then, I see no reason why you shouldn't. Mittagessen will be at half-past twelve. By the way, you'll be glad to hear that Mary-Lou has also slept well and is up as usual. In fact, she was highly indignant because I refused to let her go with the rest of the gang to Interlaken. But she's better kept quiet today. Joey Maynard has invited the pair of you over to 'English' tea and you may go. In fact," she added with a glance out of the window, "I'd advise it. When you're ready to put on your frock, come to my room and I'll do you again with the lotion and also give you a sling to keep that arm up. Oh, yes; you're wearing a sling for today. There'll be no one to see but Mary-Lou."

"All right; I'll be good," Kathie promised. "I feel heaps better this morning, anyhow, and I don't want to have to stay out of school crocked up."

"Oh, you aren't indispensable," Matron told her drily. "None of us is and we all have to find it out sooner or later. We can be spared if necessary."

She picked up the tray and marched out of the room and Kathie was left to snuggle down on her pillows again where she had another nap and finally got up at eleven.

Thanks to this common-sense treatment, she was able to appear in school next day as usual. The school, of course, knew nothing about it all. Mary-Lou had uttered lurid threats as to what would happen to anyone who gave the story away.

Lessons began as usual on the Wednesday morning— and so did something else. Kathie pulling her curtains open

120

when she was dressed, looking out to find that the snow was falling and it was still quite dark.

"It's come early this year," Biddy o'Ryan said pensively when they were all in the Staffroom, collecting their books for work.

"Don't you worry about that," Miss Moore observed. "It'll change to rain with any luck and then it'll clear off. It's far too early for the real winter snow yet."

Peggy Burnett, who had come flying up stairs to seek a bottle of lotion wherewith to massage a painful rheumatic arm about which Miss Denny had been complaining lately, overheard this and paused a moment to say, "I remember one half-term in the Christmas term when we had snow as early as this, Biddy. We couldn't go out all one day. Then we did and sculpted the most marvellous statues in snow." Then she suddenly sobered. "That was the half-term Mlle was so terribly ill and had to have a grave emergency operation. She was never well again after that."

Kathie's jaw dropped as she turned to survey the brisk and vivacious Mlle de Lachennais who was having a rapid conversation with the youngest music mistress, Mlle Lenoir.

"But she's fit enough now! " she exclaimed.

Biddy turned to look and her gravity disappeared. "Oh, goodness! I forgot you wouldn't know! " she exclaimed. " 'Twasn't Jeanne at all, at all, but our own dear Mlle Lepattre that was a partner in the school with Madame —Lady Russell. She died at the beginning of the war, but there's never a girl who was under her will ever forget her."

"Not as long as we have Tessa de Bersac in the school," put in Rosalie Dene who was with them, having brought up their mail. "She is really funny like Mlle—far more so than like her mother. And yet Mlle was as plain as they come and Tessa looks like being very pretty."

"Hello! " said another voice from the doorway.

The Staff turned with cries and Joey Maynard walked in. "I can't wait, so don't talk. I've just come to hand this over. Latch on to it, will you, Rosalie. I tried to get hold of Hilda, but she's all tied up in the study with the oddest-looking woman I've ever beheld in my life! No; I really can't stay. I've left everything every which way at home and this snow is going to get heavier as the day goes on. So long, everyone! " And she rushed away, intent on reaching home before the snow had time to thicken to a blizzard.

Rosalie laughed as she looked down at the big, square parcel. "What's this, I wonder? Well, I'd better go and get on with my job. And there goes the first bell! You folk ought to be in your form rooms and not standing about here, gossiping!" And she, too, fled.

"She's right. Come on, Kathie! You and I can't afford to leave our beauties by themselves for too long!" Biddy took Kathie's left arm and drew her through the doorway and they headed in a general exodus from the room.

Arrived in Inter V, Kathie discovered that Yseult Pertwee was missing.

"Is anything wrong with Yseult?" she inquired as she looked up to see why the girl had not answered to her name at register.

"Her mother's come to see them," Len Maynard rose to explain. "Miss Annersley sent a message for her to go to the study before the bell rang."

"I see. Thank you, Len." Kathie marked Yseult late and went on with the rest.

The bell for Prayers rang a minute or two later and when they were over, she was due for geography with Upper IV and had no time to think of anything but her work.

After break she had her own form for arithmetic and she saw that Yseult had not returned though where Mrs. Pertwee could have taken the girls with the snow falling as heavily as it now was, was a mystery.

Kathie's arm was aching badly and her temper was fraying. She looked at Con Maynard, who was almost blankly unmathematical.

"Really, Con," she said icily, "if you can't do better than this you had best go down for arithmetic."

Con's lips quivered and her eyes filled with tears, but she blinked them back and stood silent. Kathie ripped the sheets from her scribbler, handed it back to her and turned the pages of her arithmetic textbook. "You had better see what you can do with these," she said, still in that chilly tone. "Do one and bring it out to me when it's done."

Con stumbled back to her seat and dived under the desk for a moment. When she came up her eyes were suspicious but no one took any notice of her. Margot flashed a glance along the row at her triplet. She was indignant that Miss

Ferrars should have treated Con, who really did try, in this way. She finished her own work and glanced up. Miss Ferrars was going over Rosamund Lilley's work and fully occupied. Margot had in her pocket a daylight sparkler, the remains of the half-term fun. She also had a couple of matches which she had just discovered while rooting for a handkerchief. The devil that was never very far from her suggested that it would be a good idea to light the sparkler and toss it into the middle of the room. That *would* give Miss Ferrars something to grumble about and perhaps she'd leave Con alone for the rest of the lesson.

It was quite a long time since Margot had lent a willing ear to her devil, but she did so now. A minute later something raining stars in every direction shot into the middle of the room right on to Jo Scott's desk where it lay, distributing its sparks with a vim.

There was instant pandemonium. Some of the girls shrieked. Some jumped up and fled to the corners to get out of the way. Jo herself grasped in a moment what it was and picked it up, waving it over her head as she cried, "It's only a daylight sparkler. It's nothing to be frightened of! "

Naturally, this treatment sent the stars flying far and wide and there were fresh screams. Kathie herself leapt forward, snatched the thing from Jo's hand, flung it on the floor and stamped on it vigorously. The sparkler, went out in a flurry and the excitement was over.

Kathie glared round the room and the silence that fell could be felt. Those girls who had left their seats slunk back to them as fast as they could. People standing on theirs slid down and tried to look as if they had never moved. Con, between the sparkler and her sums, burst into tears. And the door opened and Mary-Lou came in with a message from Miss Derwent. Was there anything wrong? If so, could she be of any use?

"There is *nothing* wrong," said Kathie in her most repressive tones, "except that we seem to have a Junior in this form. I thought Intermediate V was supposed to be made up of Seniors. Evidently, I was mistaken."

Not very sure what to say or do, Mary-Lou stood hesitating. Kathie waited and then said, "There's nothing you can do, Mary-Lou. Please thank Miss Derwent for me."

Mary-Lou departed and Kathie was left to face a stricken

form. She was wondering how on earth Miss Annersley had not heard the noise and come in. She must be still busy with Joey's odd-looking woman.

"And just as well!" Kathie thought. "I don't want her landing on a scene like this for a second time in the term."

She turned to the weeping Con. "Stop crying, Con, and don't be silly," she said firmly. "You aren't hurt. Girls! Who threw that sparkler?"

"Me—I mean I did," Margot confessed, standing up very straight.

"Why?"

The question stunned Margot who had expected to be severely rebuked and then given her sentence. She looked round the room, completely flummoxed and finding no inspiration anywhere. Finally her gaze returned to the mistress and remained there.

"Why?" Kathie repeated, inexorably.

It was clearly impossible to tell the whole truth. Margot compromised, "Well, I'd finished my sums and I—er—I found it in my pocket and matches in my breast pocket and so—and so——" She came to a halt.

"Yes?" Kathie spoke in an interested tone, but there was an edge to it that Margot could feel.

"Well, I just lit it," she said.

"And why didn't you 'just' bring your work to me?" Kathie asked.

"You were busy with Rosamund," Margot pointed out.

"Quite so. But you could have queued up, couldn't you?"

"I—I——"

"Yes; well, you've had your fun—and upset everyone else in the room. You expect to pay for it, of course?" Kathie had come a long way since the night when Heather had let loose her toy spider and she had the affair well in hand now.

Margot flushed, but her pride wouldn't let her droop her golden head. She held it erect, gazing unflinchingly at the mistress.

Kathie thought quickly. She had a sudden inspiration. She spoke—very slowly to give emphasis to the sentence. "Very well. This is your birthday week, I think? You are going to celebrate it at home on Saturday. Your mother told me so. You three were to go home after Frühstück on Saturday morning and help your mother to prepare

124

for the party you are having in the afternoon. Len and Con may go, of course, but *you* will stay till after Mittagessen and go home with your guests."

A gasp of dismay rose from all three of the triplets. It was their first birthday in the teens and Joey had told them it was to be An Occasion. Len jumped up.

"Please, Miss Ferrars, can't you possibly let it be something else?" she implored. "Margot knows she's got to pay for her fun, but that will be punishing us two as well. Oh, *please* make it something else! We'll never have a thirteenth birthday again!"

For a moment Kathie wavered. She had never meant to punish the other two for Margot's misdeeds. Then she stiffened. She had heard plenty of tales in the Staffroom about Margot Maynard and her devil. She felt that if she gave way now, it might encourage the young lady to play tricks again.

"I'm very sorry, Len," she said, "but you can see for yourself that such a piece of naughtiness must be severely punished. The only other thing would be a Head's Report and I imagine none of you want that."

Len's face fell. She knew all too well that Miss Annersley would say that Margot deserved to lose the whole treat. She said dismally, "I see. No; that would be lots worse!" and sat down.

"But Mamma will want to know why," Con said.

"And Margot must tell her. I'm sorry for that, too, but she should have thought about all this before she played such a stupid trick. Margot, you are to write to your mother after Kaffee und Kuchen this evening, explaining what has happened, and I'll see that she gets it.

Margot was dumb. She went quickly to her seat and sat down. When she had listened to her devil she might have known trouble would be the result. Now, she not only had to miss all the fun of opening the birthday parcels with the other two, as well as helping with the preparations for their party, but she had to tell the whole story to her mother and she knew that, in the circumstances, she could look for no sympathy there. Mother would say she had asked for all she got!

"This *is* a nice prospect!" she thought as she sat struggling to keep the tears back. "I shan't be like a hostess at my own party; I'll just be one of the guests. Oh, I *hate* Miss Ferrars! She's a pig to think of such a nasty punishment. I only did it 'cos she was being so beastly to Con. We've always stood by each other. Why can't she understand instead of being so absolutely *beastly* to me?"

Chapter XV

A Visitor to Mittagessen

THERE was a stranger at the staff table for Mittagessen that day and a very queer fish she was. When the Head introduced her to the Staff at large as, "Mrs. Pertwee," Nancy Wilmot muttered to Biddy o'Ryan, "you might have guessed it! " whereat that young lady nearly disgraced herself by choking audibly.

Kathie stared at her, frankly wide-eyed. She was short, but she made up for that by breadth. In fact, she was as nearly square as it is possible for a human being to be. She wore a loose dress of bright blue trimmed with bands of embroidery, mainly in the primary colours. The corn-coloured hair she had bequeathed to Yseult was banded with a matching embroidery strip and twisted into a loose knot which lay carelessly between her shoulders. Her round and smug pink face was heavily powdered and the light eyebrows had been drawn over with a black pencil which was wearing off now. She wore strings of beads and a brooch like a breastplate in the centre of the band which finished the square neck of her dress. Her hands were loaded with rings and her wrists with so many bangles that every time she moved them, she *clanked*! Her voice was high-pitched and piercing and she used it. Oh, *how* she used it! No one else had much chance to talk when Mrs. Pertwee was present.

The Staff got very little Mittagessen that day. They were much too fully occupied in trying not to laugh. Miss Annersley next to whom she sat, was completely expressionless in both face and voice—except on one occasion—and the contrast between her trim blue frock and Mrs. Pertwee's flowing draperies was so marked as to be almost painful.

But Mrs. Pertwee was talking of the reason for her sudden arrival in the Oberland.

"Yes," she said as Elsa removed her soup-bowl before setting before her a plate of Bernerplatte. "When I knew I was going to America for so long, I felt I simply *must* see my girlies before I went. When a mother has to play the father as well, she has a terrible responsibility, Miss Annersley."

"She must have," Miss Annersley said. "Will you have some of this sauce, Mrs. Pertwee?"

"Ah, thank you, thank you. Yes; though I know you can hardly be expected to realise it yourself, not being a mother. But to be responsible for the care and well-being of three young creatures who have no one else to whom to turn is a terrible weight for one poor woman."

Miss Annersley who, for years had been responsible for the care and well-being of literally hundreds of young creatures, said exactly nothing. Mlle, sitting at the other side of Mrs. Pertwee, took it up.

"Oh, but, indeed, Madame, I can assure you that we do understand heavy responsibilities," she said in her clear, fluent English. "Figure it to yourself! Year by year we care for a hundred or more girls who, during term time, have also to look to us for care and consolation."

"Oh, but *that* is entirely different," Mrs. Pertwee told her earnestly. "They are not your *own* children. *That* is what makes the difference!"

"Oh, *why* isn't Joey here?" Nancy muttered to Biddy who was sitting next her. "It takes her to deal with a woman like this. But I understand young Yseult now," she added.

Mlle had retired, snubbed. Miss Denny, looking her grimmest, changed the subject. "And if we may ask, Mrs. Pertwee, why *are* you going to America?"

Mrs. Pertwee was only too pleased to explain. "Well, I *write*, you know," she said. "Oh, nothing *great* or likely to be *popular*. I do deprecate the modern novel, don't you? But I have made the Arthurian period my special subject and I think I may claim to know as much about it as anyone."

"But," remarked Biddy who was sitting nearly opposite to her, "surely the general opinion now is that much of the Arthur cycle is pure legend and he himself was not king of a great country, but merely a tribal chieftain."

"Oh, you are wrong there, I assure you. Arthur was a Great Christian King. But I see you know something about history." And she smiled indulgently on the school's history mistress who was an Honours B.A. in the subject.

Nancy hurriedly drank some water and swallowed it the wrong way and had to retire, choking audibly. Biddy, quite unmoved, returned smile for smile and said sweetly, "I *have* taken some interest in the subject, Mrs. Pertwee."

It was the only point in the meal where Miss Annersley's graven image expression looked like cracking. It was only for a second and luckily, Biddy made no attempt to catch her eyes. Having shot her bolt she went on with her meal and Mrs. Pertwee continued with her explanation.

"As I said before, I write," she said. "A circle of American ladies have read my latest book—well, it is hardly a *book*—more in the nature of a *brochure.*"

"They say my theories interest them extremely and they would like me to give them a course of talks on them. They offer me hospitality and a really *magnificent* fee! With my three girlies to educate and provide for, I felt I could scarcely refuse. I sail for America at the end of the month, so I decided to pop over here and see for myself that all is well with my girlies."

"If she calls them 'girlies' once more, I shall be sick!" Peggy Burnett muttered to her next-door neighbour who was on the verge of wild giggles.

As soon as Mittagessen was over and Grace had been said, Miss Annersley swept off her trying guest to the drawing-room, greatly to the relief of her Staff. Miss Derwent and Mlle stayed to supervise the clearing of the tables, for the girls were in a giggly state, too.

Mlle issued her orders in no uncertain tone—and French, despite the fact that this was Wednesday and "English" day. "Dépêchez-vous de désservir, mes filles. Alors il faut allez à Hall aussi vite que possible, tous le monde. Ne parlez pas, s'il vous plait! Déjà, nous sommes en retard!"

The girls obeyed at full speed. Yseult, having carried her possessions to the hatch, went to the door, but instead of turning to go to Hall, prepared to follow her mother and the Head to the drawing-room. Miss Derwent saw her and called her back sharply. "Where are you going, Yseult? Didn't you hear Mlle tell you girls to hurry up and go to Hall for your rest period? Go at once, please."

"I was going to join my mother again," Yseult replied.

"You must wait for that till Miss Annersley sends for you," Miss Derwent returned. "The drawing-room is her private sitting-room and you must wait for an invitation before you go there. Join the others now, please."

Yseult went off sulkily and, having seen that everything was practically cleared, the two mistresses left the Speisesaal and went to their own sitting-room where they found the rest of their colleagues laughing and talking all together.

"How long are we to be landed with *That*, Mlle?" Peggy Burnett demanded as the pair appeared.

"Me, I have no idea," Mlle said.

"Has the poor Head to put up with that sort of thing all day?" Biddy demanded. "If so, 'tis myself is sorry for her."

"She has not!" Rosalie Dene had just come in and she answered Biddy's query with her usual placidity. "This morning, she shoved her into the drawing-room with her 'girlies' and left them to it. And the good lady's catching the seventeen o'clock train to Interlaken. Jack Maynard has offered to take her to the train in his car. Mercifully, the snow's stopping. If it had gone on as heavily as it did first thing, we might have been landed with her till tomorrow."

"Thank goodness we're spared that!" Biddy said devoutly. "It's a flying visit, isn't it?"

"It has to be. She sails on the twenty-sixth and before that, she has to see to the closing of the house and arrange for the girls' Christmas holidays. She won't be back till midway through February and possibly not then. The Head's been telling her all about Penny Rest, that place Joey Maynard raves about."

"Is it that guest house in Cornwall?" Miss Armitage demanded.

"Her first idea was to leave them at school. However, the Head explained that that was impossible as the school would be closed from 22nd December to 12th January."

"Mrs. Browne will squeeze them in somehow," Biddy said with certainty. She knew Penny Rest very well and also the proprietors. "It's to be hoped though that Yseult isn't too impossible when she gets there."

"And what," demanded Peggy Burnett, "is the great idea of calling a lanky object of sixteen like Yseult a 'girlie'?"

No one could tell her and Rosalie, thinking it time to change the subject, inquired sweetly, "By the way, aren't

129

any of you interested in that parcel Joey brought over this morning?"

"Why should we be?" Nancy Wilmot asked, staring. "It was for the Head. It's none of *our* business."

"That's all *you* know!" Rosalie treated them to her blandest smile.

"What do you mean?" Biddy asked.

"Only that Madame sent the triplets' birthday presents to Joey and included in the parcel the Christmas play. Joey didn't discover until she unpacked it this morning, thinking it was only the presents. That's why she hared over with it as she did. The Head's going to read it in Hall after Abendessen tonight."

At that moment, there came a tap at the door and Kathie, who was nearest, opened it to show Elinor Pennell there.

"The telephone's ringing," she said, singling out Rosalie at once. "Miss Annersley says will you please take it, Miss Dene, as she is occupied."

Rosalie hurriedly drained the last of her coffee and stood up. "It would! Very well, Elinor; I'll come."

Five minutes later the bell rang, so the others had to depart to their afternoon work.

Rosalie came round the form rooms with notices halfway through the afternoon and the enchanted school learned between lessons and preparation that work was to begin on the Christmas play at once. As they had had none the previous year, contenting themselves with a Carol Concert, it came with an additional thrill. Only Margot Maynard was unhappy and her sisters found her in tears when they came to her after Kaffee und Kuchen in their own form room. She had her writing-case before her and was trying, in the midst of her tears, to write that awful letter to her mother.

Kathie, coming to seek a book she needed, heard her and came in. "Why are you crying like that, Margot?" she asked gently enough. "You had your fun and you knew you'd have to pay for it."

"Oh, please, Miss Ferrars, it isn't that!" Len cried eagerly. "It's just this is our real birthday and it's such hard lines on poor Margot having to write a letter like that to Mamma today."

Con, who had been looking very troubled, suddenly butted in. "It's my fault, really, Miss Ferrars."

"*Your* fault?" Kathie exclaimed. "How was it your fault?"

Con went pink, but she stuck to her guns. "Well, you see, we're triplets. We always hang together. Margot was mad because I'd done my sums so badly and you ticked me off so hard. That's why she did it. So, you see, it *was* my fault. Oh, please, couldn't you let her off just this once? She'll never do anything like that again—will you, Margot?"

"No-o-o!" howled Margot.

Kathie looked at the three of them. Suddenly she remembered what Biddy o'Ryan had said at the very beginning of things about not being too inflexible and drawing the reins too tightly. She had had no idea that this was the real birthday and, as she also knew, if she had not been feeling so poorly, she probably would not have been so severe. She made up her mind. Sitting down by the shaking Margot, she lifted the red-gold head from the desk.

"Now stop crying, Margot. You were a very naughty tiresome girl, but as it's your proper birthday, I'm going to remit your punishment this time. I think you've paid for your silliness as it is," she added, as she surveyed the swollen eyes and tear-stained face. "Len and Con, take her to the Splashery and help her to mop up and we'll let it go this time. But I shan't be so lenient again," she added with a laugh.

Margot was much too well away to stop crying at once, but there was a gleam in her blue eyes as she said shakily, "Th-Th-ank you, M-Miss Ferrars, and I'm s-sorry I was so s-stupid."

But Len had thought of something. "Will Miss Annersley agree?" she asked anxiously.

"She knows nothing about it," Kathie said frankly. "I haven't seen her to speak about it. Put Margot's case away before you go, Con. And fly, all of you. The bell for prep will be ringing in a minute."

That sent them off and Kathie, hoping she had done the right thing, retrieved her book and went back to the Staffroom to prepare her work for next day.

Chapter XVI

YSEULT AND THE PLAY

THE snow on the Wednesday had ceased before Mrs. Pertwee departed for Interlaken and the next day was fine. The two Heads made hay while the sun shone and cut out all afternoon lessons, ordaining games instead.

On the Friday, they woke up to find that it was snowing again, however, and it snowed all day, quietly, steadily and clearly meaning business.

"This has come to stay," Miss Wilson announced to Kathie who was in the mistresses's Splashery, washing her hands when the co-Head arrived to take science with the Seniors. "Ever seen a blizzard? If not, you'll know all about it before this is over. What on earth have you been doing to get such gory-looking hands?"

"My red-ink Biro leaked on me," Kathie said, scrubbing away with a nailbrush. "I put my hand in my pocket to take it out and withdrew it dripping. It gave Inter V quite a sensation!"

"I can just imagine it!" "Bill" hung up her coat after giving it a vigorous shake, removed the hood which matched it and shook that too, and then came to look at the soapy water which was red.

"Let me see. My dear girl, you can't go about with hands like that! Come with me to the labs and I'll find you something to clean it up properly. Your nails look as if you had been dabbling them in blood!"

"What a horrid thought!" Kathie rinsed the soap off, dried her hands and surveyed them ruefully. Thanks to her activities with soap and water, her left one was now as bad as the right and both were scarlet.

"What about your form?" "Bill" asked as she put a hand on the girl's shoulder and steered her towards the long passage which linked up the labs and other external buildings with the school.

"That's all right. I finished my lessons with Inter V and
132

I'm free this period. Can you really give me something to clean it up? I'll be thankful if you can. I *don't* want to go round looking like a butcher!"

"I'll fix you all right. How on earth did your Biro come to leak like that?"

"I haven't a clue. All I know is that I put my hand into my pocket and found it full of something wet and when I drew it out again it was dripping, as I said. The cap was off the Biro, but it shouldn't have made all that difference.'

"What about your coat?"

"Mercifully it was my old school blazer and that's red already so it won't show. But my hanky, which was in the same pocket, is done for. So is my blouse. I'll have to have it dyed red, for it certainly won't wash out."

Thanks to "Bill's" scientific knowledge, Kathie's hands presented a reasonably decent appearance when the bell rang for Break and she had dashed upstairs to change into a clean blouse and hunt out a woolly for the day was cold. When she went back to Inter V at the end of the morning, they eyed her apprehensively, but all was well.

"We shall get skating with any luck!" Mary-Lou told her jubilantly that night when the two sixths came to join the dancing in Hall after Abendessen. "Ski-ing, too. I'm longing for it. I haven't ski'ed for ages. I dished myself last year as you know and no one would hear of my doing anything violent all the next term."

"Where do we skate?" Kathie asked.

"On Thun. We go down after early Mittagessen and have a glorious time. But we ski up here," Mary-Lou explained. "Ever done any?"

"I've skated when I was small. We had a very bad winter and the town authorities flooded the race-course and I learned there. But I've never done any ski-ing. What is the worst snag in ski-ing?"

"Crossing your toes," Mary-Lou said promptly.

"Crossing my toes? What *do* you mean?"

"Just that! The points of the skis seem to have a fatal attraction for each other when you first learn and are forever trying to meet head on. Once you've got over that, you can manage. The rest comes with practice. I'll give you a hand if you like," Mary-Lou offered with her usual cheerful insouciance.

"Thank you. I'll remember that." Kathie had got over her antipathy to the prefect since that awful business on

133

the glacier and she was slowly learning that Mary-Lou never meant to be off-handed or impudent. A long talk with Joey Maynard on one occasion had done a good deal towards helping her. But even now, she never thought of those first weeks when she had so heartily disliked the girl without feeling that she had made a big mistake and praying that she might not make another such. It made her extra careful in her dealings with the other girls for, since she had misjudged Mary-Lou, she was afraid lest she should do it with someone else. This was to result in more trouble for her, unfortunately, though "Bill" consoled her later with the remark that it was mainly a case of growing pains and everyone had to go through them. But even that reflection wasn't much help at the actual time.

It snowed all day Saturday and all day Sunday. There was no going out at all, not even to church. No one minded that very much, for on the Saturday afternoon Miss Annersley summoned the school to Hall and gave out the parts in the Christmas play. In the evening, the two Fifths presented *Scenes from Nicholas Nickleby* and on the Sunday they were given permission to look over their parts, those of them who had speaking parts. The rest were called off for carols in the afternoon and as everyone loved singing, they enjoyed themselves down to the ground.

But on the Monday trouble began. And it arose out of a very childish desire on the part of Yseult Pertwee to shine before her fellows.

As a new girl she was naturally not entrusted with much of a part. In fact, she had exactly four lines to learn as *a lady at the court of King Herod.* It was more than a good many of her own form had, but she had learned verse-speaking for some years before she came to the Chalet School and though it was not the kind of verse-speaking the selectors liked, she did speak clearly and, after all, she was one of the elder girls in age, however poorly her work might compare with that of her own contemporaries.

Not all the Seniors had speaking parts. It was the rule that people who were facing public examinations of whatever kind in the next two terms must have as little of that as possible. Elinor, with a scholarship examination to Oxford in March, was to enact the part of the Blessed Virgin in the tableau at the end, for instance, and Madge

134

Watson with General Higher Certificate in July, was the St. Joseph.

One long part went to Hilary Bennet and another to Lala Winterton, neither of whom had anything to worry about that year. Mary-Lou was chosen for *King Herod* since she, too, was free from exams.

Singing solos went to Verity Carey whose lovely voice would have been an asset to any school, and Sue Meadows and Rosamund Lilley, both of whom had pleasant little pipes of their own.

Quite a number made up the orchestra, including Nina Rutherford and her cousin, Anthea. Nina was official accompanist to the orchestra and Anthea played the violin. Nina, gifted with a spark of genius, was easily best of all the school's musicians and was entrusted with odd rehearsals when none of the music staff could spare the time.

Yseult thought over the question long and hard. She had taken a violent fancy to the part of *King Herod* when Miss Annersley had read the play to them and she had hoped earnestly that it would be given to her. When she was passed over for Mary-Lou in the tests, she was thoroughly chagrined and annoyed. To think that she who had had verse-speaking lessons for six years should have been given just four short lines to speak while Mary-Lou, who frankly owned that she had never done anything of the kind, had a good part like *Herod* seemed to her too unfair for words. She decided to do something about it. The question was—what?

She grumbled loudly to the others over having so little, but most of them pointed out that the Staff chose the parts and then refused to listen any more. Betty Landon, who had never, with any truth, been described as tactful, went one better.

"You're new this term. Why on earth should you expect to be given a big part like *Herod* when you've only just come? Of course Mary-Lou has a better right. She's been here simply ages!"

"I have had proper experience," Yseult said stiffly.

"Well, so has Mary-Lou. She's been in lots of our plays and she's quite good. The Head and the Staff settle the parts so it's no use grousing to me about it. You go and talk to *them*, if you feel as bad as all that!"

Needless to state, Betty offered this advice in joke.

135

Never, in her wildest moments did she imagine that the other girl would be so silly as to take it in earnest. But that was just what Yseult decided to do when she had thought it over. She didn't quite dare to go to the Head of whom she stood in some awe; but she knew that her own form mistress had been called in to help with choosing for the parts. Kathie had had a good deal of experience in amateur theatricals as Biddy o'Ryan had found out, and she had been instantly called on to put that experience at the disposal of the school. Yseult went to her.

"Could I speak to you for a moment, Miss Ferrars?" she asked at the end of preparation on Monday when Kathie appeared in the form room to put a pile of corrected algebra belonging to Inter V into her drawer, ready for the next morning's work.

Kathie pushed the drawer shut, locked it and waited. "What is it, Yseult?"

It's just that I've had years of training in verse-speaking. I really am experienced and I've been in several plays, too," Yseult began, finding it rather more difficult than she had expected. "I—I thought if Miss Annersley knew this she might reconsider——"

Under the astonished gaze of Miss Ferrars, her voice trailed off into silence.

Kathie pulled herself together. "Might reconsider *what*?" she demanded, sitting down to it. "What on earth are you talking about?"

Yseult tried again. "I know, of course, that I'm new. But I do think that with all the work I've done of this kind I might have been given a better part in the play!"

Kathie was silent from sheer amazement. She had been accustomed to girls who accepted the dicta of the Staff without argument, however much they might growl among themselves. To meet one who actually went to Authority with a complaint was something so outside what she knew that she had nothing to say.

Yseult saw her advantage and pressed it. "I really do know quite a lot about acting, Miss Ferrars. I'm sure I could take on a much bigger part and make a success of it—probably better than a girl who has never done verse-speaking or acted *except* in school plays which," she was quoting her former mistress, though Kathie could not know it, "are hardly good vehicles for training in acting."

136

But this was too much. Kathie had had her own first experience in school plays and she knew that with a good producer, very excellent training can be given. "I think you must be out of your mind!" she exclaimed. "What does a child like you know about it? And what part *were* you thinking you might take?"

"Mary-Lou's," Yseult said, passing over the mistress's comments.

It was at this point that Mary-Lou herself entered the room with a letter for Kathie which had been overlooked during the sorting-out that morning. She nearly dropped is as she heard Yseult's calm claim.

"*My* part!" she exclaimed. "Well! Of all the *cheek*!"

Kathie intervened, for Mary-Lou was glaring at Yseult in no friendly way and Yseult was glaring back. "Don't talk nonsense, Yseult," she said quite kindly, but very firmly. "To begin with, you couldn't look the part——"

"I could be made up to look it," Yseult said stubbornly. "Anyhow, Mary-Lou is nearly as fair as I am so she won't look it, either. And I *know* I can play it far better than she can and that's what matters."

Mary-Lou just caught herself back from whistling at this unabashed conceit. "Whose trumpeter's dead?" she asked sotto voce.

Kathie glanced repressively at her and she coloured. "Sorry, Miss Ferrars!" Then human nature was too much for her. "But honestly, *did* you ever hear such bosh—I mean rubbish?" She caught herself up hastily. "Why, she's never even *seen* me act for we didn't give them a play this term when it was our Saturday. She doesn't know what I can do. And I'd say it if she tried to get the part of anyone else in our House," she added sturdily. "It isn't just because it's mine she's after. She *can't* know what we can do."

"That will do, Mary-Lou!" But there was very little sternness in the snub, for Kathie felt full sympathy with Mary-Lou and she, too, was rather stunned by Yseult's self-satisfaction and high opinion of her own powers.

"I've heard you read," Yseult said in a tone that showed that she didn't think much of it.

"Be silent, Yseult!" Kathie's tone really was severe now. "So far as the part is concerned, Miss Annersley has given it to Mary-Lou and that's the end of it. Now it's nearly time for Abendessen and you certainly haven't washed your hands, whatever Mary-Lou may have done. By the way, why did you want me?"

"Miss Dene found this among her own letters and told me to bring it to you," Mary-Lou said, extending the letter.

"Oh, thank you! I was wondering why my home letter hadn't arrived as usual. You may go now."

Mary-Lou left the room and Kathie turned to Yseult who was still standing there, trying to think of some even more convincing argument. "I told you to go and wash your hands, Yseult. Hurry up, or you'll be late for Abendessen," she said, her voice once more kindly. She stood up and laid a hand on the girl's shoulder. "I'm sorry if you're disappointed, but when you think it over carefully, you'll see that it was most unlikely you would be given an important part like *Herod* your very first term. Now run along."

Yseult went; but she was by no means reconciled to her fate as yet. It was clear that Miss Ferrars would do nothing about it. She must try someone else. Accordingly, she waylaid Miss Derwent next day with the same request. Miss Derwent, much more experienced than Kathie and very much more self-assured, proceeded to make mincemeat of her.

"My good girl, what you think and what the selectors think may be two very different things. We haven't all such a high opinion of your talents as you seem to have of them yourself. In any case, no one here has seen you act and I'm afraid we can't afford to take you at your own valuation. Show us what you can do with a minor part and you may have a little better one next time. And please don't brag like that! Self-praise is *no* recommendation as you may have heard. If not, let me offer the saying for your mature consideration. And now I'm much too busy to attend to you, so run along."

This soothing speech, delivered with Miss Derwent's most finished irony, cut deep, for though her work was poor, Yseult was by no means stupid. She went off smarting and more determined than ever to get that part whether fairly or not.

As she still did not care to tackle the Head, she made a final effort with Rosalie Dene who had also helped with the selections. But Rosalie had lost her usual placidity for once. Everything had gone wrong that day. Yseult could

138

hardly have chosen a worse moment to proffer her request.

"Certainly not!" she snapped. "The parts have been given out and there it ends! Don't come here, bothering me with frivolous requests, please!"

Yseult gave it up, perforce; but she had not yet given up her desire. She was a quick study when she chose and during the rehearsals, she picked up a good many of Mary-Lou's speeches. The prefect was quite good, but Yseult felt certain that she could do much better.

"She isn't nearly stately enough for a king," she thought after one rehearsal when they had to manage for the first time without their lines. "And she's not sure in those two long speeches. And she's not *nearly* dramatic enough in the bit where she has to fly into a rage. I could make ten times more of it."

Then, on the Friday night when all the Staff were having their evening coffee with Miss Annersley, Mlle de Lachennais remembered that so far the understudies for the chief parts had not been appointed and suggested that they should do it then and there when they were all together. The Head agreed and for some minutes they discussed girls to understudy the various parts. Kathie remembered Yseult's request. She had been so mistaken over Mary-Lou that she thought she had better be careful over Yseult. She didn't like the girl—for one thing, she had found her untrustworthy. Yseult was not above copying when she got the chance, or writing notes in preparation; and Kathie was convinced that she won her geography marks unfairly though so far, she had been unable to prove it.

"What about Yseult for *King Herod*?" she suggested. "She's tall and can be dignified when she likes. She also tells me she has done a lot of acting at one time and another. Her own part is very short—anyone else could take it on at half-an-hour's notice. And she has a good voice."

"I don't like her," Miss Derwent said at once. "She came to me with some sort of nonsense about being much better able to play it than Mary-Lou. Such rot! She'd never even seen Mary-Lou act then, so how could she know?"

Determined to be fair, Kathie argued it. "Oh, I know; but if we gave her the understudy, it might calm her down. Judging by what she told me it's the desire of her life to play *Herod*. She's not likely to, even if she gets the under-study; but she probably won't realise that."

In the end, after a good deal of talk, the understudy *was* given to Yseult and a very great pity it was. Kathie had made another big mistake. The wish to play the part had become almost an obsession with the girl and this confirmed it. She spent every spare moment hoping that something would happen to incapacitate Mary-Lou on the day of the play, and she watched the prefect so closely that that young woman finally noticed it and wondered what on earth was up.

"Yseult wants your part and she's considering stabbing you and hiding your body in the snow," Hilary vowed with a chuckle. "You watch out, Mary-Lou! I wouldn't go anywhere alone if I were you. You're a complete pest at times, but we're used to you now and we shouldn't like to lose you."

"Oh, talk sense! If that's all it is, I *should* worry! I thought my hair must be turning green or I was suddenly developing a limp! If it's only the silly part that's worrying her, she's had it. She may be my understudy, but I've no intention of spraining an ankle or starting 'flu just to give her a chance to rave and rant about that stage! As for you, Hilary, you're reading too many thrillers!"

The prefects laughed and the subject was dropped in favour of speculations as to when they were likely to get any ski-ing. The snow had ceased to fall several times during the past few days, but there had been little or no frost to firm it so far and though the girls *had* been outside, it had been only for prim walks along the paths dug out by Gaudenz and his henchman between the five-foot walls of snow. However, the thermometer had dropped consider-ably during the day and the girls were hoping for a chance of proper winter-sports shortly.

Meanwhile, Yseult was sadly deciding in her own mind that Mary-Lou had no intention of developing the slight-est ailment likely to prevent her taking her part. Neither was it at all probable that she would so far forget herself as to merit being deprived of her privileges like Francie Wilford, a demon of the first water.

"But I simply *must* play that part on the day!" Yseult thought wildly. "Oh, what can I do?"

"If Yseult Pertwee doesn't pull up shortly, I'm going to ask the Head if she hadn't better go down to Upper IV for my subjects," Miss Derwent remarked that evening as she scored through line after line of Yseult's essay. "She doesn't seem to have any sense at all!" And she scrawled d— at the foot and tossed the sheet on to a pile.

"If you ask me the play's got between her and her wits," Biddy remarked.

"Then the sooner it's over and finished with the better I shall be pleased." Miss Derwent snapped. "I'm sick of that girl and her airs and graces!"

"So am I!" Kathie put in her word. "Every last one of you has complained about her work to me this week and I can't help it. She's just as bad in mine and she's had extra coaching most of the term, but she doesn't seem able to understand a *thing*! Talk of something else, for pity's sake!"

"Here you are, then." Nancy Wilmot gave a chuckle. "It's to be hoped that we get some frost soon. If not, I can see things happening ahead."

"How d'you mean?" Kathie demanded.

Nancy replied with one word. "Avalanches!"

"Avalanches? But I thought there wasn't much likelihood of them till next term?" Kathie said.

"Not as a rule. But I *don't* like all this soft snow and never any frost to harden it. It wouldn't be likely here. The school and the San would hardly be up here if there was much danger. But in the Eastern Alps they get some terrible ones sometimes," said Biddy, "and the snow has been general all over Central Europe. I'm not liking it at all, at all, I'm telling ye!"

Miss Armitage got up from her table and went to examine the thermometer that hung outside a window on the landing. She came back with a wide sweet smile. "You've no need to worry. The thermometer is dropping as hard as it can go. Frost tonight, my darlings, or I'll eat my best hat!"

"I only hope you're right," Nancy said pessimistically. "I'll believe it when I see it. We've had such a weird mixture of weather this term, I'd believe anything of it."

141

Chapter XVII

HOIST WITH HER OWN PETARD!

THE frost duly came during the night and the school buzzed with excitement next morning when it got up to see the snow with the unmistakeable glassy look which hard-frozen snow always shows and which so far it had lacked.

"Ski-ing today, or I'm a Chinaman! " Emerence Hope chuckled as she scrabbled under the bed for her slippers. "Oh, goody—goody—goody! "

"What about tobogganing?" someone asked, rather unkindly, for that particular sport held unpleasant memories for Emerence.

She flushed; but she replied sturdily, "That, too. And you needn't go raking up past things like that, Heather. I know *all* about it and I don't think I'm ever likely to forget. So dry up about it, will you?"

Heather flushed in her turn. "I'm awfully sorry, Emmy! I *am* a beast! I wasn't thinking when I spoke. Forget it, will you?"

Emerence had plenty of faults, but holding grudges was not one of them—or not in these days. "O.K. Anyhow, I jolly well learned a lesson then. Do you know, I never look at Mary-Lou without saying a 'Thank You' to God because she's as fit as ever and—she might not have been." Her lips quivered though there was no one to see. That had been a terrible time when people had feared that Mary-Lou would never come round after a nasty accident she had had last Christmas term and even when she did, no one could say for a few days if she would ever walk again. Emerence had suffered deeply and Heather had had no need to remind her.

In her own little room, Kathie was regarding the frozen snow with rather apprehensive pleasure. She was longing to begin ski-ing, but she was also wondering how she would manage. She felt that too much tumbling about might be most undignified and she was still very much under the influence of her aunt's admonitions on the subject.

"If only I could get in some practice before any of the girls are about! " she thought as she brushed her hair with vigorous strokes until her head was tingling. "But how I'm to manage that is a problem. I wonder if I could slip out with my skis before Frühstück and see what I can do in the garden?"

She put her brush away just as a tap sounded on her door. Biddy o'Ryan entered immediately after, fully clad in scarlet ski-ing suit and boots.

"There you are! " she exclaimed. "Buck up and finish dressing. Put on your suit and Nancy and I will take you out and start you off on skis before the girls get going. I've just seen Rosalie and she says the Head's sent round to say that we go off after Prayers. Can't take any chances with the weather these days. Look at the sky will you? There's snow piling up there, so we'll be taking our fun when we can get it. Hurry, now, and mind you're warmly clad."

She whisked off, even as Kathie was replying eagerly, "I'll be ready in five minutes! "

As the door banged after Biddy, she dived into a drawer and hauled out her suit and wriggled into it at express speed. Her ski-ing boots, fastening above her ankles and heelless, followed. She rammed her russet brown cap on her head, caught up the matching mitts and tore off downstairs to find the other two waiting outside with her skis and sticks. Nancy Wilmot showed her how to strap on the skis and then, taking her between them, they towed her to a fairly level place where they proceeded to instruct her. By the time they returned to the school for Frühstück, all three flushed with the nip of the icy air, Kathie was beginning to get her balance though she had been stunned by the difficulty of keeping her skis in a straight line.

Word had been sent round the dormitories before the girls were fully dressed and the Speisaal presented an unwonted appearance with everyone very smart in her gentian-blue suit and the noise they made as they clumped in in their boots had to be heard to be believed!

The Head came in, extremely trig in her ski-ing suit, and Grace was said and the girls sat down to bowls of porridge, plates of fried lake fish, rolls and butter and marmalade and great cups of milky coffee.

Prayers followed and after that the school pulled on caps, strapped skis firmly, plunged hands into mitts and assembled on the drive, everyone clutching her ski sticks. People who were new to it were handed over to two old hands each and borne off between them. Kathie, knowing that her friends must attend to their own forms, and wondering what would happen to hers, found that Miss Denny had taken charge of Inter V and Mary-Lou and Vi Lucy were bearing down on her with eager offers to "slide you to the pasture land where we practice."

"Take an arm of each of us and put your feet together," Mary-Lou said. "You slide and we'll tow you. Then we'll find a quiet spot and show you what to do."

"Thank you. I only hope I can soon learn to keep my skis apart," Kathie said, with a nervous laugh. "But you mustn't stay with me all the time. I'll get the hang of it soon, I hope, and you must have your own fun."

"We'll do that all right," Mary-Lou told her. "And you'll soon be able to manage nicely. You've got good natural balance and that always helps. Ready?"

They hauled Kathie off to a quiet corner where they started her off.

"*Slide* your skis—don't try to lift them," Mary-Lou told her. "And whatever you do, do your best to keep them pointing straight ahead! "

"And don't forget to bend your knees a little at each step," Vi added. "You can't ski with straight knees."

Kathie set off, trying hard to remember all she had been told that morning, and contrived to go quite a little way before the skis rushed on each other and over she went into a snow-covered bush. The girls rushed to yank her out and get her on her feet again and then applauded her effort.

"Jolly good for a first shot! " Mary-Lou said.

"Oh, but it wasn't! " Kathie owned up. "I was out before Frühstück with Miss O'Ryan and Miss Wilmot and they kept me at it for a good three-quarters of an hour."

Kathie set to work and, by the time the whistle blew, summoning them to go back to school, she was able to go quite a distance at a time.

Meanwhile, the three Pertwees, who had once spent a winter in Scotland when there had been heavy snow and learned to ski after a fashion, had passed Mlle's test and been sent off to enjoy themselves with the rest. Ronny and Val as everyone now called them, had forgotten a good deal, but they had great fun tumbling about with the rest of the clan. Yseult managed much better and was able to look with a superior air on the struggles of Rosamund Lilley, Joan Baker and all the other tyros in Inter V as she disported herself with a good deal of assurance.

When the whistle went, the girls hurried to ski back to the path; but Yseult chose to ignore it and sped on towards the foot of the hill. Mlle skimming over the snow like a crimson-feathered bird, had to fetch her back and escorted her scolding sharply in her own tongue.

"But why did you not return at once?" she exclaimed. "You were told at Prayers that when one blew on the whistle, you must hasten to the path immediately—but *immediately*! Why, then, did you disobey? Do you not know that it may mean a fresh storm of snow coming and we must hasten to return?"

"I—I didn't hear," Yseult muttered—not altogether truthfully. She had elected to keep her ears closed to the sound.

"But you must listen. Otherwise, you must stay with the beginners."

By this time, they were tailing on to the long line heading for school. With a final indignant look, Mlle left Yseult and went forward and the girl, quite as indignant at being treated, as she told herself, like anyone as stupid as Rosamund Lilley or that silly Eve Hurrell who never seemed able to keep her feet for a minute, followed sulkily.

The snow which had caused Miss Annersley to blow her whistle, began to drift down in light flakes as they reached the gates and by the time they were in their common rooms with all the lights on, it was whirling down in a mad dervish dance that lasted all day, all night and the next day. During Sunday evening, it ceased and frost came with a wild north wind. Next day there was no snow falling and the ground was granite-hard, but such a gale was blowing that any idea of going out had to be given up. Instead of ski-ing, the girls had to buckle to at their work, to do them justice, most of them went at it with a will. They knew that when the wind had fallen if it were at all possible they would be sent out.

It was not until Thursday that the weather cleared and when it did, it was to a glorious day. The wind had dropped completely: the sun came out in the pale blue winter sky: the frozen snow glittered blindingly under his light and there was every sign that the weather would hold for that day, at least. Miss Annersley sent word round the dormitories and the excited girls could hardly contain themselves. By nine o'clock they were out and skimming over the icy ground—those of them that *could* skim, that is! —and before long they were all hard at it.

"Not the hill today girls! " Peggy Burnett had warned them before they set off. "Too many trees on either side and between the wind, the snow and the frost, some of the branches may have become unsafe. Anyhow, we won't run any risks. The men are going to make sure presently, but until we get their report, no one must go up there. We'll be safe rather than sorry, if you *don't* mind! "

No one really minded. They made the best of it and the shelf rang with their shrieks and laughter. Lady Rutherford wrapped herself up and came to stand by the fence at the back of the Elisehütte to watch the fun and admire the way in which her twins, Alison and Anthea, were progressing. Mrs. Graves, a former Old Girl and Games mistress, appeared with her small daughter, Marjorie, bundled up like a baby Eskimo and joined her, for they were good friends now. Joey Maynard arrived, pulling a small sledge on which sat the twins Felix and Felicity with their baby sister, Cecil, snuggled under the fur rugs between them. She took the baby in her arms and let Felix and Felicity tumble about close at hand. They were hardy little people and took some quite hard tumbles without a fuss.

"Quite an audience! " Miss Annersley murmured to "Bill" who had also come, bringing her flock with her, so that there were joyful reunions between sisters and cousins and old friends all over. Miss Annersley watched the excited girls with smiling sympathy which changed to annoyance as she called out, "Yseult—Yseult Pertwee! What are you doing? Look where you're going and be careful! You'll have someone down if you try to rush about like that! "

Yseult pulled up as soon as she could and moved off in another direction. very red and embarrassed. The truth of the matter was that the silly girl had let her desire to play Mary-Lou's part so completely master her sense and decency that she had been half-trying to engineer some sort of a mild accident to that young woman. It had struck her that among so many people who seemed unable to keep

146

their feet for more than five minutes at a time, it could be easily done. If Mary-Lou came down and sprained a wrist or ankle, she would be out of the play. And who could say that it was anything but a simple accident? With this in mind, she had been literally barging across the pasture to where the prefect was flying along with half-a-dozen others. Kathie was beginning to come along quite well and she had ordered off her self-appointed teachers to have some fun themselves while she did her best alone.

Yseult had reckoned without the eagle eye of the Head and she moved off disconcerted. In fact, she gave up the idea for that time and the chances are that she would have finally let it go, however much she objected to her part in the play, if it had not been for an incident that occurred that evening.

It was the rule of the school that only prefects among the girls might use the front staircase, what Sybil Russell had once grandly called "the *hoi-polloi*" contenting themselves with the back staircase. It was a rule that was rarely broken, but this evening Yseult found at the beginning of preparation that she had come down without a handkerchief and went off to get one. Miss Ferrars had pulled her up for the same thing earlier on in the day and when the girl was coming out of her dormitory, she was dismayed to hear Kathie's voice near the head of the school stairs. Rather than face a second scolding for being careless, Yseult made for the front stairs which were close at hand. She was halfway down when Mary-Lou, who had been to the Head to collect a batch of essays, came from the corridor into the entrance hall and caught her.

"I thought," the prefect said in her rather stilted German, "that you knew that you are forbidden to use the front stairs? Go back and come down by the back ones, please. Oh, and take an order-mark for breaking the rule."

Yseult would have argued it, but she heard the sharp tap-tap of Mlle's French heels. She looked very sulky and did as she was told; but Mary-Lou's calm authority had roused her worst feelings and she went to bed determined to get what she wanted somehow.

The chance for the "somehow" occurred in the afternoon next day when the girls were out again. Gaudenz, having examined the pines crowding along the slope of the hill, reported them all safe. The girls who could ski had been told they might use it and received the news with enthusiasm.

Mary-Lou, having clambered to the top, was flying down when Yseult, circling about by herself, happened to be near. Without giving herself time to think, the silly girl dived forward at the utmost speed she could manage, hoping to crash into the racing prefect as she descended. Mary-Lou was an experienced ski-er by this time. She saw, as she thought, Yseult coming along without bothering to look up and she swerved neatly to avoid the other girl. Yseult, not nearly so practised, was unable to stop her mad flight and she ended up by crashing into the trunk of the last pine, striking it with her left shoulder and turning a complete somersault to land flat on the hard snow.

Mary-Lou swung round again and came flying to the rescue by which time Yseult had struggled to a sitting position and was sitting clutching her left arm, tears of pain streaming down her cheeks.

"Oh, you poor dear!" the prefect exclaimed. "Are you awfully badly hurt?"

By this time, Miss Burnett, Miss Wilson, Miss Annersley and Kathie, who had had no idea she could manage so well, had all come up and Peggy Burnett had wrenched off her skis and was kneeling down to examine the injury as well as she could for Yseult's wraps. She looked up at last.

"Well?" "Bill" demanded while Miss Annersley, who had likewise discarded her skis and was crouched down, supporting the weeping Yseult, while the rest of the Staff kept the other girls from crowding round, looked at her anxiously.

"I don't know certainly," Peggy said in rapid German, "but I rather think it's a broken collar bone. We'd better get her back at once. Oh, Joey!" as that lady, having pushed her daughter into Lady Rutherford's arms, came tearing up, "Is Jack at home?"

"He ought to be now. What's she done?" Joey demanded.

"Collar bone gone, I think. I can't make sure. She may have just put it out. Anyhow, we want Jack. Can you fly back and tell him? We'll look after your babies.

"You'll have to do that, anyhow. I'm turning the sledge over to you to get her along. It's small but adequate and much the easiest way of moving her. And take her to our house and I'll scoot off and get a room ready and warn Jack." She stopped over Yseult. "Don't howl like that, Yseult. Every time you sob you're shaking yourself and making it hurt more. We'll soon have you put to rights— don't you worry! "

The next moment she was skimming over the ground with the same easy, graceful movements the girls admired so in Mlle and some of the other experienced ski-ers. The sledge was pulled up to where Yseult sat, and she was got on to it and drawn carefully to Freudesheim with "Bill" supporting her and Mlle and Miss Annersley pulling, while the other mistresses either took charge of Joey's babies or set the girls on to ski-ing again with the assurance that Yseult was not badly hurt, only they wanted to get her to bed quickly to recover from the shock.

Ronnie and Val accepted this and went off though they were not quite so wild as they had been and the school was kept going for another half-hour. Then they had to return to school or they would be late for Kaffee und Kuchen. Arrived there, they were met by Rosalie Dene who told them all to hurry and change for the evening.

Kaffee und Kuchen was nearly over when the Head came at last with news. Yseult had indeed broken her collar-bone and, in doing so, had not only put an end to any idea of her playing *Herod,* but was also out of the play altogether. It would take place in ten day's time and she could hardly be *a lady of the court of King Herod* with her arm in a very modern cage.

Poor Yseult! She had certainly been hoist by her own petard!

Chapter XVIII

THE END OF TERM

IT was the last full day of term. The girls were all packing with Matron and all the Staff in charge. Any language might be talked and most rules were in abeyance. Form rooms had been cleared up that morning and left in immaculate order, ready for cleaning during the holidays. Mary-Lou and Hilary Bennet, with Miss Ferrars in charge, were going through the library books. Miss Derwent was checking off all the acting-cupboard possessions and seeing them packed neatly away till they were wanted again and had delegated Kathie to attend to both libraries.

"Well," said Mary-Lou at last, "that's the last of the fiction. How many books missing, Hilary?"

"Five—one John Buchan which is down to—who did you say, Miss Ferrars?"

"Blossom Willoughby."

"H'm! Not so good! Blossom's a prefect and ought to set a better example," Mary-Lou said severely.

Hilary laughed. "Except in games, you can't expect an awful lot from Blossom. Fine her well, Miss Ferrars, and we may be able to get another book extra!"

"What an immoral remark!" Kathie said, joining in her laughter. "Very well, Hilary. I quite agree with Mary-Lou that she ought to set a better example. Now what else is missing?"

"Well, *August Folly* by Angela Thirkell—and I rather think that Miss Andrews has that. It's not entered anywhere, but I seem to remember she got it out last Saturday. She said she wanted something soothing after all the excitement of the play and I told her to help herself and I'd put it down later. Then there are two of the *Daneswood* series and *At the Back of the North Wind* from the Junior library and that's the lot. Two of the Thirds are responsible for the *Daneswood* books and Rosamund Lilley gave the other to me this morning and I forgot to bring it along.

It's in my locker. I'll just go and fetch it and rout out the others and then we're all square."

"Very well. If you'll do that, Mary-Lou and I will go on to the Reference books and you can join us as soon as you've collected these others. Come along, Mary-Lou." And Kathie got up, handing the catalogue over to Hilary and the three left the Fiction library, intent on their duties.

"Miss Ferrars," Mary-Lou said when they were in the room dedicated to the Non-fiction section, "may I ask you something?"

Kathie, sitting down at the table, turned to look at her. Mary-Lou's voice was unusually serious. "What is it?"

Mary-Lou perched herself on the table. "Well, I hope you won't think I'm being cheeky or anything like that, but I *would* like to know what I did at the beginning of term to make you dislike me so much. I've often wondered, for I couldn't think of anything. And since half-term, of course, it's been all right. But what *did* I do?"

Kathie flushed. "I think it was—not understanding you. You seemed so—offhand in your manner and treated me as an equal. I hadn't expected it. We didn't do that sort of thing at my school and—well, there it was."

The red crept up into Mary-Lou's face now. "My stupid manner!" she said mournfully. "I've heard about it over and over again since I came to school. The others thought it was probably that, but I couldn't see that I'd treated you any differently from the way I treated other people and—well, there it was."

"Yes; I see that now," Kathie assented. "But you must admit that you can be rather a shock at times and it was my first term, teaching. However, as time went on I began to see I wasn't the only one. Then—well, you know what happened at half-term. Also, I was getting more experience and that helped."

"It did, I suppose. And you have been a big help in lots of ways. You are so awfully *fair!* " Mary-Lou said with the frankness that could still be a stunning shock to Kathie. "Oh, by the way, I'd like you to know that Yseult had it out with me yesterday."

"Had *what* out?"

"Oh, you know! The play business! "

Kathie looked at her thoughtfully. "Mary-Lou, what about that accident of hers? Did she say anything about it?"

Mary-Lou went red again. "How did you know? I'm jolly sure Yseult's said nothing to you and I know I haven't and I don't suppose anyone else noticed."

"I happened to be watching you," Kathie said shortly. "It struck me that it wasn't just clumsiness on Yseult's part, though, of course, I've said nothing to anyone else. But did she try to bring you down?"

"She didn't say so," Mary-Lou began.

"I don't suppose she would—or not directly. What possessed the silly girl?"

"A mad yearning to play *Herod*, I think. She told me she'd tried to get the part, anyhow. No one would hear of it, she said. Then she was chosen to be my understudy and that seems to have settled it for her—why what's the matter?" Mary-Lou wound up in consternation, for Miss Ferrars was looking stunned.

"Then it was *my* fault! " she exclaimed.

"*Your* fault? How could that be? The understudies are settled by the selection committee."

"Yes; but I suggested her. I knew how badly she wanted the part. I'd made such a bad mistake about you, I began to be afraid I was making a mistake about her. So I proposed her as a kind of consolation prize."

"Yes, but that didn't mean that she'd get it unless the others agreed," Mary-Lou argued. "And it certainly didn't mean that anyone could expect her to become so obsessed that she'd play a dirty trick like that. Anyhow," she grinned broadly, "it didn't come to anything. In fact, she chucked herself out of the play altogether by it. I don't see that you're to blame at all. You only suggested her and anyone might have done that."

"Yes; I suppose so," Kathie agreed slowly. "All the same, Mary-Lou, take warning by all this if you're going to teach——"

"I'm not! I'm having another full year here and one at St. Mildred's and then I hope to go to Oxford. After that, I want to go in for archeology. And here comes Hilary! Come on, old poop! You've been an age over collecting those books! "

"Had such a time finding Miss Andrews," Hilary explained as she joined them. "However, I got her in the end and now the Fiction is complete."

The Reference library was much more quickly dealt with. Only one book was missing—a geographical Reader, which was eventually tracked down to Ailie Russell who blandly referred Mary-Lou to her eldest sister, Sybil, when a fine was duly demanded of her.

"You see," she explained, "I drew nearly everything out of my Bank Saturday before last when we went down to Interlaken to Christmas-shop. And I haven't anything left of my pocket-money, either. So you'll *have* to ask Sybs for it—or let me go on owing it till next term."

"Oh, *what* a brat she is! " Sybil exclaimed when Mary-Lou came to her. "I've a jolly good mind to tell you to let her owe it, only Mummy is so down on us for that sort of thing. Josette's never been half the bother she is! " She fished in her bag and produced a franc note. "Here you are! But just wait till I get hold of Miss Ailie! I'm not going to go on doing this sort of thing as long as I'm at school. And Josette shan't have to take it on, either. I'll *larn* her! "

"The fruits of being the elder sister! " Mary-Lou grinned as she took the note. "All the same, you're quite right. It would serve young Ailie right if you did leave her to owe it. Then she'd have to be reported and either Miss Derwent or Miss Ferrars would have to take it up—I say! " with a complete change of tone. "I've just discovered it! Those two can rhyme! "

"*What?* What are you talking about?" Sybil demanded.

"Don't you see? How thick of you! 'Derwent' can become 'Derry' and the obvious short of 'Ferrars' is 'Ferry'! " She intoned gaily, "Derry and Ferry were two pretty men'. I can't finish it. I don't know how it ends. Let's see." She thought rapidly. "Of course! Here you are, a nice new couplet, free gratis!

'*Derry and Ferry were two pretty men.*
They went off to bed when the clock struck ten'

How's that for genius?"

"Rotten! " Sybil retorted. "Don't be such a mad ass, Mary-Lou! "

In the Staffroom the Staff, relaxing a little after a day's hard work, were gossiping among themselves. Kathie, sitting at her table which she had just cleared, was silent, listening to them. She was going over the term in her mind and thinking that she was quite glad Mary-Lou had cleared the air for both of them that day. She had made some bad mistakes, but she had also learned her lesson. She had found that there is no need to stand stiffly on your dignity at all times and she had also discovered that friendships between Staff and pupils are quite possible, especially with the elder girls. The business of the triplets' birthday had taught her that it does *not* do to hold the reins too tightly and that it is well to go to the root of matters before you condemn people out of hand.

"It's been a good term on the whole," Nancy Wilmot suddenly proclaimed out of the blue. "We've had fewer alarms and excursions than we frequently do——"

"What about young Yseult?" Sharlie Andrews demanded.

"Oh, just what you might expect with the sort of bringing-up she's had. I expect we shall find next term that she's settled down to being an ordinary schoolgirl and no more bother than most of them are. Anyhow, we get a rest from her, though I'm sorry for the Brownes if I'm wrong about her."

"I'm not worrying," Biddy said placidly. "Penny Rest will put paid to all her worst antics. And the two kids are quite decent little souls."

"What do *you* think about it?" Nancy asked, whirling round to Kathie. "You're being very silent. Join in the natter and tell us whether you think we're right about young Yseult? Will she have improved by next term?"

"Oh, I think so," Kathie replied, roused out of the reverie into which she had fallen. "I don't see how she could help it. And oh, but I'm thankful we have no play to worry about next term. That Herod business was a complete worry!"

"Oh, she'll have to learn she isn't the only pebble on the beach," Miss Derwent said serenely. "That's really what's been wrong with her from the start. Mary-Lou was really amazingly good. And as for no play, have you forgotten that we have the St. Mildred pantomine coming along?"

"No; but that's not really our business. St. Mildred people run it and *they* choose the people they want to fill in. Miss Nalder told me all about it when we were having Abendessen after the play last week. *We* have the Sale to worry over——"

"That's all you know." Rosalie Dene had arrived in their midst. "I've just come to inform you all that the

Heads and Madame have decided to take Joey's advice and shunt it on to the summer term so that we can have it in the garden."

Cries of dismay greeted this.

"But we've *always* had it in the Easter term!" Mlle exclaimed in her own tongue. "How, I ask you, are we to keep the girls occupied if we have no Sale?"

"Oh, there'll be plenty to do. The Seniors have to finish their exam work and we can keep the rest hard at it for the term," Miss Denny said cheerfully.

"Not to speak of the fact that next term is bad weather term and we may expect snow and frost and, as a result, ski-ing, bob-sleighing and skating," put in Miss Moore. "Besides, it gives them all more time to fill their stalls. We were sold out a good hour before the end last year. We must all pitch in when we come back and try to have as much again. And think of the lovely competitions we can have if it's a garden show!"

"Well, I must get back to the office," Rosalie said with a yawn "I only came to tell you the latest and to say the Head wants us all to have coffee with her after Prayers. What are the girls doing now?"

"Musical Questions," Peggy Burnett laughed. "Some-one's written a story using the titles of pieces of music. Elinor's reading the yarn and Nina's playing the music when it comes and they have to fill it up. A good time was being had by all when I came past the Hall. Anyhow, Abendessen will be ready in another twenty minutes and the Juniors and Junior Middles go to bed after that and the rest at nine because of the long journey tomorrow. We needn't worry about them, thanks be!"

Rosalie nodded and went back to finish up some work. She and the Heads would be staying on after the others to clear everything up, but the more she got through now, the sooner it would be all done. The rest decided that it was time to tidy up for Abendessen and drifted off to their rooms. No one could change on last night as only their travelling things were not packed. Kathie washed her hands and face, brushed her hair and powdered her nose and then went downstairs to the office to hand in her Christmas address. She had had a letter that morning, saying that the Graysons had decided to go away for the week so she must hand over the new address.

"Well," Rosalie said as she took the slip and filed it, "you've been here a term now. What about it?"

"Oh, I love it!" Kathie told her. "I wouldn't be anywhere else for all the tea in China! I'm looking forward to the holidays. I've never been away from home for so long all at once before this; but I'm looking forward to next term, too."

The elder woman—Rosalie was in the middle thirties—smiled at her. "That's good hearing!" she said heartily. "We like to keep our mistresses, you know. Well, there goes the bell! Come along for the last Abendessen of term."

But Kathie's greatest thrill came later on in the evening. The girls were all in bed and Matron, who had slipped out of the drawing-room to make her rounds had come back to announce that everyone was either fast asleep or on the verge of it. As Frühstück took place at half-past seven next morning to permit them to catch the special train to the valley which was always put on for their benefit at the end of the Christmas term when the roads might not be safe for the motor coaches, this was as well. The Staff gave themselves up to another half-hour of chatter and relaxation and Miss Annersley, rising from her seat beside Mlle, came over to the corner where Kathie happened to be alone at the moment.

"I want to speak to you, Kathie," she said, smiling. "You have been on trial this term and I think you will like to go home tomorrow knowing that you've come through with flying colours."

"Oh, Miss Annersley!" Kathie was pink with confusion and delight. "But I have made some dreadful mistakes, you know."

"My dear girl, you wouldn't be much use to us if you didn't. It's by our mistakes we learn if we've anything in us. And, another thing, it's the people who make mistakes and try to profit by them who have most sympathy with their fellow creatures. Go on as you've been doing and I prophesy that you will be exactly the kind of mistress the Chalet School most wants and needs. Now I'm going to send you all off in a minute, for you've to be up early as well as the girls. We shall have very little time in the morning, so I'm going to say goodbye and give you my Christmas wishes now. A very happy Christmas and good

156

holidays to you and a joyful return next month when we start work again!"

"Thank you, Miss Annersley. I hope you'll have a good Christmas, too. And though I'm longing to be at home and see the home folk again, I'll be delighted to come back next term and d g in again. You know," she added as they both rose to go, "when I think what I've heard from some of the people I was at Oxford with and contrast the sort of school life they have with mine here, I can scarcely believe my luck—especially when, as I told Auntie when Rosalie's letter came last holidays, it was the wish of my heart to come!"

"Ah," said Miss Annersley, laughing, "but then, you see, this is the Chalet School!"

THE MILLIONAIRE'S HANDBOOK

Peter Eldin

A treasure trove of money-making schemes . . .

Cash-in on –

Car-washing

Budget-planning

House-minding

Bait-breeding

Bulb-growing

and many more ideas for getting rich quick. It'll be your best-ever investment!

Armada

THE AWFUL JOKE BOOK

compiled by Mary Danby

The best of the worst! Here is a great new
collection of ghastly gags, hideous howlers,
riotous riddles and witty wisecracks –
illustrated with scores of hilarious cartoons.
You'll drive your family and friends
round the bend! Here are a couple of
examples . . .

What is the main ingredient in dog biscuits?
Collie flour.

NEW COWHAND: What is the name of this ranch?
RANCHER: The Lazy G Triple Diamond Circle S
    Bar Z.
NEW COWHAND: How many head of cattle are there?
RANCHER: Not many. Only a few of them survive the
    branding.

Armada

CAPTAIN ARMADA

has a whole shipload of exciting books for you

Here are just some of the best-selling titles that Armada has to offer:

- ☒ **The Palomino Mystery** Ann Sheldon 90p
- ☒ **The Millionaire's Handbook** Peter Eldin 85p
- ☒ **The Mystery of Smugglers Cove** Franklin W. Dixon 85p
- ☒ **Calculator Fun and Games** Ben Hamilton 85p
- ☒ **Pony Puzzles** Charlotte Popescu 80p
- ☒ **The Mystery of the Moss-Covered Mansion** Carolyn Keene 85p
- ☒ **Mill Green on Fire** Alison Prince 85p
- ☒ **Biggles, Pioneer Air Fighter** Capt. W. E. Johns 90p
- ☒ **5th Armada Crossword Book** Robert Newton 85p
- ☒ **Mystery Stories** Enid Blyton 85p

Armadas are available in bookshops and newsagents, but can also be ordered by post.

HOW TO ORDER
ARMADA BOOKS, Cash Sales Dept., GPO Box 29, Douglas, Isle of Man, British Isles. Please send purchase price of book plus postage, as follows:—

> 1—4 Books .... 10p per copy
> 5 Books or more .... no further charge
> 25 Books sent post free within U.K.

Overseas Customers: 12p per copy

NAME (Block letters)

_____

ADDRESS

_____

_____

_____

While every effort is made to keep prices low, it is sometimes necessary to increase prices on short notice. Armada Books reserve the right to show new retail prices on covers which may differ from those previously advertised in the text or elsewhere.